VIP

Battle of the Bands

VIP

Battle of the Bands

By Jen Calonita

Illustrated by Kristen Gudsnuk

Peachtree

LITTLE, BROWN AND COMPANY
NEW YORK   BOSTON

Text copyright © 2016 by Jen Calonita
Illustrations copyright © 2016 by Kristen Gudsnuk

Little, Brown and Company

Hachette Book Group
1290 Avenue of the Americas, New York, NY 10104
Visit us at lb-kids.com

Little, Brown and Company is a division of Hachette Book Group, Inc.
The Little, Brown name and logo are trademarks of Hachette Book Group, Inc.

The publisher is not responsible for websites (or their content) that are not owned by the publisher.

First Edition: July 2016

Library of Congress Cataloging-in-Publication Data
Names: Calonita, Jen, author. | Gudsnuk, Kristen, illustrator.
Title: Battle of the bands / by Jen Calonita ; illustrated by Kristen Gudsnuk.
Description: First edition. | New York ; Boston : Little, Brown and Company, 2016. |
Series: VIP ; 2 | Summary: Twelve-year old Mackenzie "Mac" Lowell accompanies her favorite
boy band, Perfect Storm, on another road trip and chronicles her experiences on tour.
Identifiers: LCCN 2015037258| ISBN 9780316259774 (hardback) | ISBN 9780316259767
(ebook) | ISBN 9781478909729 (audio book) Subjects: | CYAC: Diaries—Fiction. |
Bands (Music)—Fiction. | Popular music—Fiction. | Automobile travel—Fiction. | Friendship—
Fiction. | Diaries—Fiction. | BISAC: JUVENILE FICTION / Girls & Women. | JUVENILE
FICTION / Performing Arts / Music. | JUVENILE FICTION / Social Issues / Adolescence. |
JUVENILE FICTION / Social Issues / Friendship.
Classification: LCC PZ7.C1364 Bat 2016 | DDC [Fic]—dc23
LC record available at http://lccn.loc.gov/2015037258

10 9 8 7 6 5 4 3 2 1

RRD-C

Printed in the United States of America

Book design by Michelle Gengaro-Kokmen

To Lisa Gagliano, for many reasons, but especially for that time she tried to win me a jacket worn by Joey McIntyre of NKOTB

LOCATION: SoundEscape Recording Studio—New York City

I, Mackenzie Sabrina Lowell, do solemnly swear on Perfect Storm's potential world music domination that everything I write in this journal is the truth, starting with this:

I'M IN A RECORDING STUDIO LISTENING TO PERFECT STORM RECORD THEIR FIRST FULL-LENGTH ALBUM!

Me!

I'd pinch myself to make sure I'm not dreaming, but then I'd wind up with a welt that turns black and blue and forces me to wear a jacket in May. Instead, I make lists.

MAC'S TOP FIVE REASONS WHY THIS IS GOING TO BE THE BEST SUMMER EVER:

1. Mom is taking me back out on the road with Perfect Storm when school ends. Since it'll be my summer break, that means no Krissy tutoring sessions! YES!

2. No school also means Scarlet and Iris can come with Jilly and me to some of the tour stops. (Iris says this can only happen if she and Scarlet pool their babysitting money and stop buying PS shirts, but my fingers and toes are crossed!)

3. Being on the road means steering clear of Jones Beach. Mom usually drags me there at least twice a week in the summer, even though we all know the ocean has sharks. But there'll be no time for the beach when we're on tour, so I'm saved from a possible shark attack for another year! YAY!

4. Extra time on the tour bus means more time for me to finish my *Mac Attack* comic book! I've already got a third of it done from our last road trip. This time there'll be no annoying distractions (like essays on the generals of the American Revolution. Yawn) to keep me from my artistic dreams.

5. Touring with Perfect Storm means I get to spend more time with my crush, Kyle Beyer! Let me write that glorious name a few more times: KyleBeyerKyleBeyerKyleBeyer. Sigh... I could say his name all day! It's *that* dreamy. Just like Kyle!

"COO-COO-CA-CHEW!"

My pen with the fuzzy pink monster topper drew a long, jittery line at the sound of the bizarre birdcall. I'd been hearing that sound over and over all afternoon.

3

"CAW! CAW! CAW!" Perfect Storm's producer, The Raven, crowed again with full-on bird flaps to emphasize his excitement. His birdcall was so loud that I thought the glass window separating us from the band was going to shatter into a million pieces.

That's exactly what happened in *The Sharkinator*

Returns. My friends and I watched it during a sleepover last night even though Mom begged us not to. In *The Sharkinator Returns*, though, the glass in an aquarium shattered and the sharks attacked a group of high school kids on a field trip and… and…I think I blacked out after that.

"Is this guy serious with the bird bit?" Scarlet whispered to Iris and Jilly.

"It's so annoying," Jilly agreed. Her dad is Perfect Storm's manager, so she's met a lot of music producers, but I was pretty sure The Raven had to be the strangest yet. "And you thought Einstein was weird with all his 'scientific formulas' for making a hit song."

Jilly said bands like Perfect Storm work with a lot of different producers when they're doing an album, but I was starting to miss Einstein and his crazy beats. He had a weird name, but he looked normal and stuck to human language. The Raven looked like a bird with his black hair, big nose, and wiry, thin body; and the twenty-one-year-old was even dressed head to toe in black like, well, a raven. I wasn't sure ravens crowed, though. Didn't they just hang out around cemeteries and look scary?

"Perfect Storm's tracks are blowing the roof off this joint!" The Raven said to Jilly's dad. "This bird hears a number one single!"

Suddenly, I felt an overwhelming sense of pride. PS was killing it in this studio session and had been working for ten hours straight (I'd only been here for two). Inspired, I let out a bird-call of my own, even though I'd never made a sound like that in my life.

"CA-CAW! PS RULES!" I cheered. There was silence. Then I heard PS laughing through the speakers. I quickly sat back down as The Raven gave me his best evil-villain glare. "Sorry. I got carried away."

"I am the only one who speaks during recording sessions," The Raven said stiffly. "I need silence to reflect on the band's energy."

I leaned closer to the girls, squeezing Scarlet against the padded walls. "It won't happen again," I whispered. I already knew The Raven didn't like us "Storm Chasers" being there, but that was TOO BAD. We were invited!

"The girls are just excited," said my mom.

Or as I now refer to her: THE COOLEST MOM IN THE ENTIRE UNIVERSE (even the parts that aren't discovered yet). And here's why: A few months ago, my mom gave up her desk job to become Perfect Storm's tour manager, and she took me along for the ride.

"Understood, but absolute silence is key in a recording studio," said The Raven. "My baby birds are learning to fly in there. This is not really a place meant for children."

"Hey, Mac!" I heard my name amplified through the sound system before I could complain about being called a child. Heath Holland was grinning and waving at me through the glass. "We're really digging that birdcall you just made," he said. "Think you could record the sound for us to use on our song 'The Story of a Girl'? It's going to be the first single off our new album."

The Raven frowned. "I really don't think it's strong enough for a single. As I've said before, my pick is definitely 'Bring Back the Sun.' I co-wrote it and..."

The Raven was ruining my moment! "I'll record the sound!" I stood up, pushed my way past the girls, my mom, and Briggs to reach the bendy microphone that The Raven was holding and practically yanked it out of his hands.

"Great," said Zander Welling from inside the studio booth, on the other side of the glass. He ran a hand through his wavy curls that were always falling in front of his electric blue eyes. "The caw sounds like a girl's scream, like the kind we hear

8

at concerts. But make it louder, with more feeling, this time."

"Um, Mac?" Jilly said quietly. Whatever she wanted could wait. PS needed me!

"Add in some different bird sounds, too," Heath suggested. "Maybe an ostrich or a pterodactyl?"

"A pterodactyl?" Zander repeated.

"Yeah," Heath said pointedly. "The dinosaur bird thingie. Go for it, Mac."

I looked back at my friends triumphantly. Jilly was mouthing something, but I closed

my eyes and took a deep breath. "COO-COO-CAWWWWWWWWW! SCREECH!" I added The Raven's bird-wing flap for effect.

Heath and Zander applauded, but the person I most wanted a reaction from was holding his head like he had a headache.

Kyle, Perfect Storm's sensitive British guitarist and now songwriter—aka my *current* crush and seventh-grade Spring Fling date—was staring at me. His soulful brown eyes make me envision a future in Paris together. I'll write comic books in an apartment with a view of the Eiffel Tower while Kyle sits at the other end of our shared desk and writes awesome songs that are about me and a life filled with lots of berets and amazing cheeses. (Jilly says Paris is all about cheese.)

"NICE!" said Heath. "That caw is the techno vibe we've been missing!"

"I'm confused," The Raven said. "What's happening?"

Briggs leaned over and spoke into my mic.

10

"Boys, I think you're getting a little loopy from all that time in stale air. Maybe we should take a break."

"After Mac records the sound, Briggsy." Heath grabbed a green guitar the same shade as his current hair color and motioned for me to come into the recording booth. He strummed the strings and hummed my caw sound. Zander joined in. "Now your turn, Mac!" I watched Zander hold up his iPhone and point it directly at me to record.

Kyle jumped up. "Don't do it!" Heath and Zander groaned. "They're trying to make you the victim of their latest YouTube video."

OH. My face heated up like I'd spent too long in a hotel hot tub. I was seconds away from being a YouTube joke called Bird Girl. "Ha!" I laughed weakly. "Almost got me." I backed away from the glass as Kyle gave me a sympathetic nod.

"It would have been perfect," Heath moaned. "She was flapping her wings and everything."

11

He demonstrated, and I could see that his arms were covered in new fake-tattoo sleeves.

"Break time!" Briggs announced, and The Raven threw down his notes and left the room. "Take fifteen and then we'll try to finish this song within the hour. You guys have an early morning tomorrow with that Z100 interview."

The boys went out the back of the recording studio, while my mom and Briggs walked off talking about all the tour stuff they had to get done before we went back out on the road again.

My friends were sympathetic. Iris pulled me in for a hug. Her reddish-blond hair smelled like strawberries. "The guys like you enough to prank you and let the whole world watch! That has to be a good thing."

"I wish Heath pranked me," Scarlet said, looking longingly at the recording booth that was now empty. Her expression quickly turned sour. "Not that I ever would have fallen for that joke. Seriously, Mac. I thought you knew the guys better than that."

Scarlet has never been one to sugarcoat things like Iris.

"I tried to warn you." Jilly jumped into The Raven's now-vacant producer's chair and gave it a spin. "Didn't you see me mouth 'Don't do it'?"

"I thought you were saying 'YES, do it'!" I grumbled. "Now I've humiliated myself in front of Kyle by flapping like Big Bird."

"I don't think Big Bird actually flaps," Iris pointed out. "Doesn't he have really small wings?"

"He's way too big to fly," Scarlet agreed. "He'd never lift off the ground."

I was still huffy. "My point is, I looked ridiculous instead of cool and fun like I was at the Spring Fling."

"Not the Spring Fling recap again!" Scarlet slapped her head, and I noticed that her black and gray nails looked exactly like Heath's. He loved to borrow our nail polish and paint his

13

nails funky colors. "Mac, we love you, but how many times are we going to do the play-by-play?"

Okay, so maybe I typed up a minute-by-minute report of Kyle's and my time at the dance together and pulled it out every few days to recap it again. (Example: 6:57 PM KYLE: *Wow, this gym is a scorcher! Is the heat on in here?* ME: *No, it's always this hot.*) Was it a bit much? Maybe. But can I help it if I like reliving the single greatest night of my life? "You guys don't know what I was going to say," I complained.

Jilly pulled her gum out of her mouth and raised her hand like we were in the middle of a school session with Krissy, who's in Los Angeles for the summer tutoring a Disney Channel star instead of us. "You guys had so much fun, but you've become good friends and you don't want to ruin that by Kyle thinking you want to be more than friends..."

"If your mom wants to ruin your life by saying you're too young to date your future husband, then it's pointless to even think about having a boyfriend…," Scarlet added.

"But when you're older, you can totally see the two of you settling in Paris and eating croissants every day…," Iris finished.

"Ooh! Ooh!" Scarlet started jumping around. "You know what Mac hasn't brought up today? How Kyle wrote her—"

"—A SONG," the three of them said in unison.

I was getting annoyed now. "Can I help it if I'm excited the boy I want to move to Paris with wrote a song about me? I mean, if Kyle didn't like me, he wouldn't have written me a song. Right?"

"YES!" the girls said in unison again.

"Whoops-a-daisy!" someone said in a British accent I knew all too well. "I'll come back later."

I slowly turned around.

Oh no. Oh no. Oh no. Oh no.

I felt like I swallowed a surfboard (which a shark did on *The Sharkinator Returns* last night. It wasn't pretty).

Kyle was standing behind us, and I had a feeling he'd heard every word I had just said.

**LOCATION: Home (hours after
I tried to be Bird Girl)**

When the boy you like hears you gushing about him, you tend to panic.

Maybe that's why I picked up the closest thing to me—my journal—and threw it at Kyle's head for no good reason.

"OUCH!" Kyle touched his forehead where my glittery journal had struck him. I saw a red welt begin to spread.

"Kyle!" I rushed toward him, forgetting all about my journal, which was now lying on the floor. "Are you okay? I'm SO sorry."

"I'll go see if the studio has a first aid kit," Iris suggested, and rushed out the door.

"I'm fine. It's just a bump." Kyle looked at me curiously. "Why'd you throw your journal at one of your best mates?"

"I thought you were an intruder," I lied. "I was trying to protect my friends." If Kyle wasn't convinced, he didn't say. I looked down at our sneakers. The white toes were practically touching. "So, did you happen to hear what we were talking about?"

Pleasesaynopleasesaynopleasesayno...

"All I heard was you yelling, but you do that a lot." Kyle gave me a cheeky grin that made me feel like a bowl of Jell-O. "Did I interrupt anything?"

"Nope," I said as Iris burst back in with an ice pack.

Kyle took it and held it to his head, leaning against one of the control panels, with its hundreds of buttons. I liked the green army jacket he had on over a white T-shirt. I think he wore

it in PS's last video. I loved that video. The guys were walking along a wharf on a windy day, and Kyle's blond hair was blowing in his eyes and...

"Mac? Are you okay?" Jilly waved a hand in front of my face. Everyone was staring at me, and I felt my palms begin to sweat.

"Fine!" I laughed like a hyena. "Sorry, I was just thinking about a movie I watched." Why couldn't I be cooler, like Mac of *Mac Attack*, the comic book I draw in my spare time? I gave her my name, but we didn't have much else in common. As the leader of a crime-fighting girl band, she always said and did the things I only dreamed of saying and doing.

Kyle started to laugh. "Not *The Sharkinator Returns* again? I still can't believe I let you talk me into watching that movie last night. It was bloody awful!"

"It's educational," Iris said solemnly as the rest of the band walked in, carrying chips and Roaring Dragon energy drinks. "How else will we know what to do if a shark bursts through a sink drain?"

"One hour to go!" Briggs announced. "Nail this song once and for all and you guys are done for the day."

"Then we can eat?" Heath asked, offering Scarlet a chip from his bag. Scarlet started to giggle uncontrollably. "These snacks will only hold me for so long. I'm STARVING."

"Do you guys want to get dinner with us after?" Kyle asked me.

KYLE JUST ASKED ME TO DINNER. Even though he had already seen me through the glass for hours and talked to me during breaks at the vending machine, he still wanted to spend more time with me. I could see the City of Light in the distance and us walking along the Seine River...

"I think we're heading to Little Italy," Kyle said. "I've still never been." Kyle loved exploring cities. He was the best tour guide I knew other than Jilly, who could remember street corners and addresses for restaurants she hadn't been to in years.

"I've never met a chicken parm I didn't love," I said. "Count us in." We smiled at each other for what felt like a long time until Heath interrupted.

"Hey, Mac," he called. "I'm out of chips. Can you call for a snack delivery? CAW! CAW!" Zander joined in, and I glared at them both.

"All right, chums, that's enough," said Kyle.

"Look at that. He's defending your honor, Mac," Heath added. "He's such a good bloke. My apologies for messing with your lady, mate!"

I felt like I was about to burst into flames. Which may be why this is the first and last time I will ever write these words:

I've never been happier to see Lola Cummings.

The tall, model-like blond I'd dubbed Big Bird came crashing through the studio doors with her entourage in tow. My friends and I weren't fans of Lola, but since she was the daughter of the guy who created the Wave One radio app that sponsored most of Perfect Storm's gigs, we had to put up with her. Briggs and my mom had to fawn over her a bit, but the rest of us tried to keep our distance. Lola had her bored-looking nanny, Amber, with her, since at fifteen she still couldn't travel by private jet alone. HA! Her annoying friend Bridget, who always wore her hair in a braid and chewed gum like a cow, was back, too. As much as I hated having her around, Lola did make a good distraction from this awkward moment with Kyle.

"Your number one fan is back, boys!" Lola shouted at the top of her lungs. "I missed you guys SO much!" She ran straight to the band, kicking my journal across the floor. I started to lunge for it but got distracted by the glittery, bedazzled PS shirt Lola was wearing. I recognized it from one of the fan sites. The thing cost more than twenty album downloads. "Did you guys miss me, too?" she asked the boys, hugging each of them. "Tell me you missed me! I know it's been weeks since I was here, and I'm sorry," she said with a glossy pink pout.

"Wait, when did you leave?" Heath asked. "I didn't notice."

Scarlet and Iris snorted, and I noticed Lola's eyes became serpentlike slits. She quickly recovered, wrapping herself around Heath. "Oh, Heath!" she said with a laugh. "That is why I love you. You're SO FUNNY!" She snapped her fingers, and Bridget and Amber started to laugh, too. Heath looked very confused. Poor guy. "So, what did I miss? Are you done recording? Can we hang?" She gave me a look. "Unlike some people in this room, I don't have a curfew."

The Raven started squawking. "Who are these three?" he asked as Bridget popped another piece of gum into her mouth and blew a massive pink bubble in his face. "Are they staying, too? This is not a good environment for finding the boys' center of truth through song. I need quiet to record."

"Lola, make yourself comfortable," Briggs said as my mom ran over to soothe The Raven's nerves. "We can make room so you can hear the guys' recording session."

"If you need room, maybe the little kids could leave." Lola batted lashes that were as thick and curly as I wished mine were. Mom had a no-makeup rule, too, so the most I got to wear was the occasional swipe of lip gloss. Lola gave me a look. "Shouldn't you be in school?"

"Shouldn't you be?" Jilly shot back. She pulled her hair up in a bun, as she usually did before she did something physical. Normally that was some sort of sport, but at the moment, I was pretty sure she was getting ready to knock Lola out. Iris stepped forward as backup, her arms raised in a tae kwon do stance I remembered from one of our recent classes, while Scarlet gave her best moody stare. The one her mom says she has 85 percent of the day now.

"No, it's a staff-development day," I snapped, and immediately cringed. That made me sound even younger than I am! Why couldn't I just say no and leave it at that? Mac Attack would have known what to say the first time around.

Amber and Bridget laughed. "She is so cute," Bridget said.

Cute. That word needed to be banned from the dictionary unless it was being used to describe a puppy in a pink basket or a chunky baby in a puffy diaper.

Lola pretended to pinch my cheek. "It's like Take Your Daughter to Work Day! Maybe if you're good, your mom will take you out for ice cream after."

Think Mac Attack. Think Mac Attack. "Actually, we're going out to eat with the guys after they finish up." I gave her a smug grin. "They invited us. Maybe you're not their number one fan after all."

Lola's bronzed cheeks fell slightly before she leaned in so only I could hear her. "I guess they needed someone to fawn over them while I wasn't here, but now that I am, you can step aside. Go home, little girl." Lola walked over to Kyle while I fumed. "Kyle and I need time together so he can write me a song," she said loudly. "I hear he's become quite the songwriter."

"He's got two songwriting credits on the album already," Heath said as Zander texted alongside him. His phone sounded like a slot machine in Las Vegas. "Tomorrow we record this rocking song he wrote, 'The Story of a Girl.'"

"A song about Mac," Jilly gloated, and Kyle and I both turned a shade of purple associated with grape juice. "I'd say that makes her number one in the guys' book."

"The song is about *Mac*?" Lola sounded stunned. She glanced at me ever so briefly before lifting her arm off Kyle's. "Is it a nursery rhyme?" Amber and Bridget laughed again. The rest of us didn't. "Now it's time to write a song about a real girl, not a kid. What do you say, boys?" Lola looked to Heath and Zander, but neither of them was paying attention. Heath was too busy snacking, and Zander was still texting. It was a beautiful thing to watch—Lola Cummings being totally ignored. "Zander? Z? Want to write about your favorite girl?"

"The band is my someone special. I don't have time to date right now," he said on autopilot, as if he were being interviewed. Now it was the girls' and my turn to laugh, causing Zander to snap out of it and look up from his phone. "Huh? What are we talking about?" He spotted Lola, and his eyes widened. "Lola! Hey! When did you get here?" Bridget's bubblegum bubble burst with a loud pop.

Lola tried weaving her arms around him. "Zander! Can you write your number one fan a song?" I could see Iris's jaw set. Even I was ready to breathe fire. My crush on Zander may have ended when we were on the road this spring, but there was no way I was going to let someone like Lola sink her claws into any of my favorite band members, which was all of them. "We can talk about it over dinner and shopping tonight. My treat. What do you say?"

Zander pushed a lone curl out of his eyes. "Sorry, Lola. We already have plans with Mac, Jilly, and their friends. Rain check?"

Hee. Hee. Hee.

"Oh, okay. I just thought, since you hadn't seen me in a few weeks,

you'd drop your plans." Lola was getting more flustered by the moment. She side-eyed me again, and I couldn't help but grin as wide as possible. I'm sure I looked like the Joker.

"Sorry," Zander said as his phone started to ping some more. "How long are you in town? Maybe we could do another night."

Double hee. Hee. Hee.

"What?" Lola was used to getting her way. "I mean, don't you think your reservation should include your number one fan?"

"Oh, it does," Zander said, missing the question again. He pointed directly at me and flashed a grin so bright that Amber got weak in the knees and had to be caught by Bridget. "Our number one fan is Mackenzie Lowell!"

Score!

Zander high-fived me, then bounded back into the recording booth, and this time I had my Mac Attack attitude ready and waiting. Thankfully, Mom and Briggs were both on their phones, so they couldn't reprimand me for being rude to their sponsor's daughter. "Jilly, how many times did Zander and the guys say I was their number one fan?" I prepared to count on my fingers.

"TONS!" Jilly replied gleefully.

"They also didn't invite Lola to dinner or take her up on her shopping offer." I looked at Lola's friends. "I think you guys are out."

"Don't forget the fact that they've never written a song about Lola," Jilly practically sang.

"You babies—SMACK!—can't talk to—SMACK!—us like this," Bridget said in between gum chewing. "Without Lola's dad, no one would have even heard of Perfect Storm!"

"I don't get what's going on here." Lola was shaking. "I feel like I'm having a nightmare or a migraine or both!"

"Maybe you should go back to your hotel and lie down, then," Jilly suggested, nudging the bewildered girls to the door. "It's not like you have plans for dinner!"

The two older girls were fuming. I noticed Bridget clutching her oversize slouchy bag to her chest like we were going to rob her. She probably had Zander's jacket in there. She was always stealing the band's clothes. Then Jilly locked the door behind her and high-fived us.

YES!

When we all left the studio together a little later, there was no sign of Big Bird or her friends. Briggs and Mom were ahead of us, talking about some big Lemon Ade show the boys were asked to open for Memorial Day weekend, while the girls and I followed along behind our favorite tired-looking boy banders.

"Towel? Roaring Dragon? Gum? Refreshing face spray?" Iris held up her bag of post-recording-session must-haves. She'd been working on the kit for a week. "Whatever you need, I'm sure I have it."

"Sour cream and onion potato chips?" Heath asked.

"Spaghetti with meatballs?" Kyle seconded.

"Someone to answer my tweets for this contest I stupidly decided to throw without asking Piper's opinion first?" Zander grumbled.

"Ooh! I can do that!" Scarlet snatched Zander's phone away. "Let me be 'you' so you can rest. I know exactly how you'd answer your tweets anyway. I read every single tweet you guys write!" Scarlet's fingers flew across the screen, and Zander actually looked relieved.

Just then, we heard a shout from down the hall. "Cody! Look! It's them!"

A door opened ahead of us, and two guys wearing T-shirts with lightning bolts on them came running out. They had the same nose, brown eyes, and dark hair. They were clearly brothers.

"Dude! *Dude!*" the older-looking brother kept saying, and I tried not to laugh. I knew what it was like to meet Perfect Storm for the first time, and these guys were obviously excited. "I'm Jeremy, and I'm a HUGE fan." He pumped Zander's hand. "This is amazing. Dude! Amazing! It's totally fate that you're here tonight. Meet my brother, Cody."

"Hey, man," Zander said with a yawn, shaking hands with Cody, who seemed to be around my age. "How are you? Did you guys want a picture or an autograph? We were just heading out."

"Autograph?" Jeremy questioned. "No, we're artists, too. Look!" He and his brother turned so we could see the backs of their T-shirts. There were clouds and lightning bolts on the back, too, along with two words. "We're Thunder and Lightning. We're the most intense part of a storm. It's an ode to you guys, dude!" He hit Zander in the arm.

"Can they do that?" Zander asked Kyle, frowning. I could almost see his brain working.

Jeremy's eyes widened. "Would you guys

want to come hear us record our demo? It's for your label! They want us to be the next you!"

"Are we going away?" Heath asked the others, and Jilly laughed.

"No, no; I mean, *like* you," Jeremy said, getting flustered. "They want another group like you, so we're hoping our demo kills it. We're torn, though, about what song to record for them."

Kyle ran a hand through his hair, and Heath exhaled. They hated disappointing fans, but I could tell they were shot, and listening to more music was the last thing they wanted to do.

"Sorry, guys, they've been here for hours," Jilly jumped in, sounding like her dad. "They have to go. Good luck, though."

Jeremy put out his arm. I think it was to stop Zander from walking by, but Zander whipped out the Sharpie he always had in his pocket and wrote on Jeremy's wrist. "You want an autograph? No problem! Good luck in there."

"Wait! Can't you guys hang for one more minute?" Jeremy tried again, running in front of them. "We really could use your opinion."

"Please?" Cody asked, his voice softer than his brother's. "This could be our big break. We've never made a demo."

"There's always a first time," Zander said with a smile. "I'm sure you'll pick a winner. Good luck!"

"Best of luck, mate," Kyle added as he passed.

The girls and I followed, and I watched Jeremy's expression change from über fan to cranky fan. I'd seen this happen before. Everyone wanted something from PS, and there just wasn't enough time in the day for the guys to please everyone.

I could hear the two brothers as we walked down the hall. "I can't believe they couldn't come in to hear a few track picks," Jeremy said.

"It's okay," his brother responded. "Thunder and Lightning is going to be huge without Perfect Storm's help."

"You're right. Forget those dudes," Jeremy grumbled. I glanced back and saw him trying to rub the signature off his wrist.

"Good luck!" I called to them in a cheerful voice, even though I thought they were being a bit rude.

Jilly gave a deep sigh. "That is why I could never be a rock star. Everyone wants a piece of you."

I'll say. The guys were mobbed again outside the recording studio, at the restaurant in Little Italy that didn't even know we were coming, AND on their way back to the hotel that night. Me? No one even looked at us on the train ride home.

I was so tired that it took me until I was brushing my teeth to remember I never picked my journal up after I threw it at Kyle's head. As soon as I realized it was gone, I got jittery like Mom does when she has too much coffee. The second she got off the phone with Briggs, I begged her to whisk us back into the city to break into SoundEscape Mac Attack–style and rescue my diary.

But Mom surprised me. "Looking for this?"

She held out my blue sparkly journal. "I found it down the hall from the studio when I ran in for my phone charger. You must have dropped it out of your bag by accident. You should be more careful."

I hugged the journal tightly to my chest. "I know. I'll never let it out of my sight again," I vowed. And I meant it.

Ladies, they're ready for you onstage.

Great! They'll be right there!

I'm so excited to be working with you all.

We're looking forward to working with you too, Lindsay.

Remember, you have that interview following the show and then you have two more tomorrow morning and a radio call-in and...

FLA FLIP

Chillax, Linds. We've got this covered. Don't worry.

Let's have fun with the show first.

I can't wait to play our new tunes!

New tunes? No one told me you have new songs! We need to publicize them and...

Lindsay, try to enjoy your first Mac Attack concert, okay? You need a **break.**

FLIP *FLIP*

MAC ATTACK ITINERARY

But...but...this is my first night as your publicist. It has to be perfect!

Excuse me, ladies. Right this way.

Into the elevator that will take you down to stage level.

FWISH

What's going on?

YOU WON'T BE PLAYING ANY NEW SONGS AT YOUR CONCERT, MAC ATTACK! ROBOTIC MOMINATOR WILL SEE TO IT YOU DON'T EVEN MAKE IT TO THE STAGE!

You won't get away with this, Robotic Mominator.

I ALREADY HAVE. THAT ROADIE WAS NO ROADIE. HE'S ONE OF MY MINIONS AND THIS ELEVATOR IS RIGGED TO STAY LOCKED UNTIL I GIVE THE SIGNAL FOR IT TO PLUMMET TO THE BASEMENT. ENJOY YOUR RIDE, LADIES!

I just got this job! I don't want to plummet to my death!

No one is plummeting anywhere. We need to think.

The escape hatch has been tampered with. It's bolted shut.

The doors are rigged. Something is keeping them locked.

I can find a way around that.

A nail file? How is that going to save us?

Watch and learn, Lindsay.

Saturday, May 28

I have to write this down because I don't think Future Me will believe it happened: I'm spending the weekend at the beach.

I've never been a sand-in-your-hair, zinc-oxide-on-your-nose kind of girl. I don't drink or eat anything on sand because it can easily get in your soda can or your turkey sandwich with provolone cheese, spicy mustard, and extra pickles (my favorite). Cheese puffs are out, too, because your fingers are sandy, which means they're going to ruin the puffs. It's a cheese-puff tragedy waiting to happen.

And yet here I was at the Jersey Shore, which is known for its boardwalks, funnel cakes, beaches, and occasional shark sightings. (Gulp.) Briggs wanted to be somewhat near Atlantic City to hear some new band play at a casino, so he rented a house in his favorite New Jersey beach town, Stone Harbor. Jilly invited Scarlet, Iris, and me to come with her. May in New Jersey is usually still too chilly to go in the water, but my friends and dozens of others were braving the fifty-degree water temperature to do it. It helped that it was eighty and sunny out.

Except me. I was sitting on a lounge chair working on sketches for my *Mac Attack* comic book while I watched Jilly, Scarlet, and Iris boogie-board from a (safe) distance. It's not like the soft breeze was annoying when it blew my notebook around. And the heat certainly wasn't getting to me. I read somewhere that it's good to sweat. My stomach wasn't growling at the sight of the hoagies that were just delivered to the beach. Boogie-boarding with the girls didn't look fun, either. Not. At. All.

Cough.

I watched Jilly catch a wave that she rode all the way in to shore. She effortlessly stood up, unhooked the boogie board strap from her wrist, and jogged toward me, carrying the board under her arm like a pro. She's my most athletic friend.

Jilly wiped the water away from her face. "Aren't you hot?"

"Does my red face give me away?" It was sweltering under my umbrella!

"Walk down and dip your toes in the ocean." Jilly gave me a fierce look. "I promise there are no sharks here."

"They can swim in shallow waters," I pointed out. "I've read it online."

Jilly rolled her eyes. "Not *that* shallow." She grabbed my hand with her wet one and pulled me up. She was really strong for such a petite girl. "We're going to be able to fry an egg on you if you don't cool off."

"I'll go in up to my ankles, but only if we're in front of the lifeguard stand." In shark movies, it was always the person swimming too far from the lifeguard who got eaten first.

Jilly ignored me and led me down to the water. I had to admit, the closer we got to the ocean, the cooler I felt. Kids flew by us on boogie boards, rode waves, or drifted around in tubes. The sound of their happy squeals was interrupted only by the occasional whistle. The guards seemed super strict here. Surely, they'd spot a Sharkinator if a fin were circling the area.

Iris and Scarlet came splashing toward me, kicking up water as they ran.

"Attention, all sharks! Mac is in the water. I repeat, Mac is in the water!" Scarlet wiped her wet face with the orange surf shirt she had on over her bathing suit and staked her boogie board in the wet sand. She'd written PS IS MY LIFE! on the bottom of her board.

"Look, she's in up to her knees," Iris pointed out. She was still wearing her tie-dye goggles. She hated getting water in her eyes. "If you can handle that, you can definitely try boogie-boarding next!"

The water must have pulled me out. I wouldn't walk into the cool ocean myself, would I? Then a kid on a boogie board crashed into me, sending me into the water on my hands and knees where—

"OUCH!" I jumped up and ran back to the shoreline. "Something bit me! Everyone, look for fins."

"You probably hit a piece of broken shell." Scarlet sounded unsympathetic.

"Be daring, Mac," Jilly encouraged me. "Think of PS. I'm sure the guys are doing something exciting in the Bahamas. Don't let them show you up!"

Perfect Storm was in the Bahamas with Lemon Ade, playing at some resort. I could only imagine the thousands of Lola look-alikes hanging on the guys. They were probably having the best time. Was I really going to mess up my own because of a silly fear of sharks? There were dozens of people in the water. Half of them were under the age of ten, and they didn't look worried about a shark eating them for lunch.

"I'll do it!" I rushed back to the water before

I could second-guess myself, grabbing Scarlet's board and paddling out. I could hear the others cheering, but I was concentrating on not looking down. If I didn't see how dark the water was, I wouldn't worry about what was lurking beneath the surface. Jilly paddled up next to me.

"I thought you'd like some company," she said, turning her board back to shore to wait for a wave. We were in up to our shoulders at this point, and I was trying hard not to panic. The shore looked so far away, so I was grateful to have her there. "Scarlet ran to get her phone to video your big moment. The minute the wave starts coming toward us, start to paddle. The wave will catch you and pull you to shore. Got it?"

"Got it," I said, and not a minute too soon, because I could feel the water pulling backward and the wave beginning to form behind us. It looked HUGE.

"One, two, three, GO!" Jilly shouted, and the two of us began paddling. Seconds later, I could feel the wave pushing me forward, past kids playing in the water until—WHOOSH!—I was sliding on the sand.

"I did it!" I shouted. The four of us jumped up and down, screaming like we just met PS for the first time. The lifeguards were looking over, but

I didn't care. "That was awesome!" I wiped the sand and water away from my face. "Let's do it again!"

"You need to get your own board," Scarlet pointed out. "You didn't buy one, remember?"

"I think her exact words were 'I'd rather see Perfect Storm get the chicken pox and cancel their next five concerts than buy a boogie board!'" Jilly reminded me.

"That *was* a little harsh," I admitted. "I'll get one and come back."

"We'll all go," Jilly said. "We could get frozen custard. Or fudge. Or both!"

I laughed. "More fudge is fine by me. But if we're all going into town, then maybe we can also do something else I've been dying to do."

"Are you going to make me play mini golf on that rooftop?" Jilly asked. She was afraid of heights.

"Nah," I said as we walked along the boards

that led us back to the streets where one beautiful home followed another. "I don't want you throwing up on me. I was hoping we could try a psychic." Jilly groaned. "It could be fun! There is one right by the frozen-custard stand. We could all get readings."

"From a beach-town psychic?" Scarlet lowered her shades and gave me a skeptical look. "It's going to be bogus."

"You don't know that," I said. Lemon Ade, who PS opened for this spring, had a psychic reading in at least three tour stops. She said it really helped her channel her chi, whatever that is. "Madam Celeste has been in business for twenty-four years." According to her sign. "It could be fun to hear what she thinks Future Us will be like."

Jilly shrugged. "I guess I'm game."

Iris nodded. "Me too."

Which is when Scarlet caved. "Fine, but I'm not believing a word she says! They're all frauds."

I'm not sure Scarlet would still use the word "fraud" after hearing her future as predicted by Madam Celeste. She learned that she's destined to be a famous inventor. ("Madam Celeste said my braces-that-don't-look-like-braces idea is going to be HUGE!" Scarlet squealed when she emerged.)

Iris wasn't as happy with her report. It said

nothing about her winding up with a "tall, dark haired, brooding artist with the first initial Z." Even after prompting Madam Celeste several times during the reading. Iris came out looking dejected. "She said I'm going to live a long life and karma will always be on my side."

I don't know, but that seemed like good news to me.

Jilly was equally uninspired. "She sees green in my future, and me living a very comfortable life." She shrugged her sunburned shoulders. "I already knew that. My dad is loaded." Her eyes wandered over to the fudge shop across the street.

My Madam Celeste idea was turning out to be a bust. It sounded like she was a fraud. Her shop was sandwiched between the custard place and a funnel-cake stand. When I walked in, I saw she was wearing what looked like a Halloween gypsy costume. Her makeup was super caked on, too,

with bright red lips. When I sat on the folding chair across from her, she looked at me strangely.

"You, dearie, are in for a storm," she said, pointing a long red nail in my direction. "A perfect storm at that."

My ears perked up. Maybe Madam Celeste was the real deal after all! She knew about Perfect Storm! "Yes, I am!" I said giddily, leaning forward and pulling out my phone. I couldn't help but show her the picture I drew for the guys' album of a ship in a stormy sea. "My art teacher says I have talent." I looked into her gray eyes. "By any chance, do you see the Eiffel Tower in my future?"

Madam Celeste frowned. "I do not understand. You have seen this storm you will face, too? Perhaps you have the gift, like I do. It is in your eyes."

"Gift?" I was confused. "Who is getting me a gift? Is it someone whose name starts with K, because—"

Madam Celeste clasped my hands. Her palms were ice-cold and white. "You have dark days ahead of you. You may have already been betrayed and don't even know it. A perfect storm is coming for you, and you cannot stop it." Her stony stare disappeared and was replaced by a small smile. "That will be twenty-five dollars, please."

I pulled my hands away and reached into my wallet for payment. What did she mean by a perfect storm if she didn't mean my favorite boy band? "That's it?"

Madam Celeste pulled out a black money box and opened it to make change for my two twenties. "I see what I see."

Friday, June 10

Madam Celeste was wrong, wrong, wrong! HA! The last couple of weeks were anything but stormy. In fact, they were sunnier than ever (literally—it has been sunny almost every day this month).

Things were going great. Perfect Storm was back in town, having survived their trip to the Bahamas without getting stranded on a desert island with pretty fans in bikinis. (This was a recurring nightmare I had Memorial Day weekend. I blame the psychic reading.) And while I suffered through the remaining weeks of school in a hot classroom, PS was close by in New York

City, recording more tracks for their album. Heath had texted me yesterday that they were finally supposed to record "The Story of a Girl" track next week after making some tweaks to the music and lyrics with The Raven, who still didn't think it was strong enough to be a single. If The Raven ruined the first (of hopefully many) songs Kyle wrote about me, I was going to go Mac Attack on him.

As Mom and I stepped out of a cab at Central Park, the sun was just beginning to rise over the trees. I stretched my arms and loudly yawned.

"Wake up, sleepyhead!" Mom said as she placed a lanyard over my head. I stared at my favorite words in the whole world: VIP BACKSTAGE ACCESS. I've kept every pass from every concert I've been to with PS. This one had Perfect Storm's faces outlined in the stars and stripes associated with the *Good Day USA* logo. "Getting up at five is worth it to see Perfect Storm perform live this morning."

"Definitely!" I half yawned, half yelled. PS was appearing on the *Good Day USA* morning-concert series, which was a huge deal, and it meant Mom had to be there super early to make sure everything was ready for their set.

"Briggs said the boys are on their way. We can wait for them backstage." Mom walked slightly ahead of me through Central Park, typing a message on her phone as she talked. "The concert is only about a half hour, and then they're off to the studio to record while Briggs and I finalize their future tour plans," she added. "Lemon Ade's tour is winding down, so we're trying to decide if they should take a break from the road till they can headline or co-tour with someone else who is also just starting out."

"Take a break from touring?" I freaked. "I can't live without Perfect Storm all summer!"

"Breathe, Mac." Mom steadied me. "I suggested they finish their album first, but the label wants them on the road at the same time to keep the momentum going." Mom pushed a strand of hair behind her ear. "You'll be packing again before you know it—lighter this time," she stressed.

I might have overpacked a teensy bit last time. "It's summer. Shorts and tees take up less room."

Mom walked through the security check

ahead of me. The concert area was directly past security and packed with girls carrying PS signs and wearing PS shirts. They were singing along to a Perfect Storm song playing from the speakers on the stage in the middle of the park. There was a huge banner that said PERFECT STORM LIVE THIS FRIDAY MORNING ON GOOD DAY USA hanging overhead. A cameraman was getting a close-up of the girls while another was focusing on the morning-show host, Raquel Rodgers. When she gestured to the crowd, a crew member onstage held up a sign that said SCREAM, and the fans went nuts. Mom and I were ushered behind the stage to a series of tents, one of which said GREENROOM.

I know the word "tent" sounds like something you'd find on a Girl Scouts camping trip, but these were luxury tents that looked like rooms in someone's house. The greenroom for Perfect Storm was HUGE! There were couches, a coffee table filled with breakfast snacks, and a makeup table and chair. They had even set out

67

potted plants and a carpet to cover the grass. A drink fountain filled with Roaring Dragon gurgled in the background (thankfully, it was the red energy drink, not the green one I accidentally sprayed all over Zander one time. He's deathly afraid of all edible green things). At the moment, we were the only ones in the room.

Mom's phone started to ring. "I have to take this, but you can wait here." She dashed out, leaving me alone with all that makeup. I rushed over and began trying black eyeliner. It went on a little crooked, but it made me feel very Mac Attack. I added pink gloss to my lips so they were super shiny like Lemon Ade's. I even smacked them in the mirror for effect. *Mwah!* I looked pretty good! Raquel Rodgers probably got her hair and makeup done twice a day. I could get used to that. Maybe I was destined to be a morning-show host.

"Hi, I'm Mackenzie Lowell, and this is *Good Day USA*," I said with a cool accent into the makeup mirror. "On today's show, we have the hottest boy band on the planet: Perfect Storm!" I cheered. "I have the exclusive on the band's upcoming tour, what they're like when they're not recording, and…and…" What else could I add? Ooh, I knew. I could ask who they were dating. "And…"

"Who is the cutest?" someone asked.

I was so startled I jumped and sent eyeliner pencils, makeup brushes, and lip glosses flying. "Kyle!" I dropped to the ground to hide my tomato-red face and began picking up the makeup. "You snuck up on me again." Kyle walked over to help. He smelled like maple syrup and soap. I stopped what I was doing for a moment to breathe the scent in deeply. Maybe a little too deeply. And loudly.

"Are you okay?" Kyle put a hand on my arm.

"I'm fine!" I said. "I just thought I smelled a fire. I wasn't sure if someone left a curling iron on. I'd hate for Central Park to burn down because of someone's need for curls."

Kyle looked ready for summer in a lime-green T-shirt and jeans, his hair styled to keep it from moving in the wind. "I don't smell anything." He grinned, and I felt my heart go KA-THUMP. "I'm sure you're just imagining things, but if you're not, I promise to rescue you from the flames."

How sweet! I could see Kyle carrying me out of the smoky tent to safety...

"I said, do you want the chocolate chip?" Kyle asked. He was holding out a plate of muffins. "I know it's your favorite, and it's the only one they have."

This is what happens when you daydream. I had missed Kyle's offering me my favorite

70

muffin. Double sweetness! "You can have it. You need your energy."

Heath came barreling into the tent playing air guitar. Today his hair was orange, and it was super messy. "There's a Roaring Dragon fountain! Cool!" Heath took the muffin from

Kyle's hand. Kyle and I looked at each other and shrugged. Heath bit into the muffin and offered us the rest.

"Dude, that's gross!" Zander said as he walked in. He grabbed the muffin remains and tossed them like a hot potato. Kyle caught it and shot it at Heath, who threw it at Zander's head. "Watch the hair! These curls have already been locked in place." Zander shook his awesome curls, which I had to admit were still mesmerizing.

"Not bad for seven AM, Zander," Jilly teased, appearing in the tent at the same time as Briggs.

Briggs was already on his phone like Mom. It took me a second to realize they were actually talking to each other from opposite sides of the room. They quickly hung up to talk in person. Then the room got really loud as makeup artists and *Good Day USA* members flooded in to mic the guys and check their faces for shine. Jilly and I ducked out to keep from suffocating.

"This is way too early for me," Jilly said with

a yawn, and I noticed she was wearing the same leggings I saw her in the night before.

"Mom had me up at five," I said, "but it was worth it. Usually I have to watch the *Good Day USA* concerts from my living room before I leave for school and then DVR the rest."

"Daddy says it's a big deal that Perfect Storm was asked." Jilly swiped a bagel from someone walking by with a tray. "'I Need You' is still climbing the charts, so I guess it got them noticed."

"Excuse me? Can I get one of those?" I saw a familiar dark haired boy running after the guy with the bagel tray. The guy ignored him. "Excuse

me? Bagel? Want? Please?" He stopped in front of us, and his shoulders drooped. "Figures. Perfect Storm arrives, and suddenly no one else exists."

It was one of the fans from the studio who was recording his demo last month.

bagels...

"Cody, you didn't catch him? I need my carbs before we go onstage!" The other boy came running over in a black-and-white varsity jacket just like his brother's. It was too matchy-matchy.

"He just kept walking." Cody gestured to the

retreating figure that was now heading into the Perfect Storm dressing room.

"Of course. Our names aren't Zander, Heath, or Kyle, so we don't deserve breakfast," Jeremy said with an eye roll. "I can't stand Perfect Storm. Those jerks think the world revolves around them."

Jerks? Hating my favorite boy band? I'd heard enough. "Hey!" I poked Jeremy in the shoulder. "Don't talk about Perfect Storm like that."

"Mac," Jilly said calmly. "It's not worth it. Just ignore them." She was used to this sort of thing, having been around PS longer.

"No! You can't trash PS like that, especially at their own concert," I said.

"Who are you? Their manager?" Jeremy looked at me intently and started to laugh. "I recognize you. You're the little fans who were at the recording studio that night we were there. Of course you'd take their side. You don't know any better."

"And you're that brother duo we met called…" Jilly snapped her fingers. "Thunder Clap?"

"Thunder and Lightning," Jeremy and Cody said at the same time.

"Weren't you stalking PS that night?" Jilly asked suspiciously. "You wanted them to listen to your demo choices, right? And now you hate them?"

"Yeah!" I chimed in because I had no clue what else to say.

"We *used* to like Perfect Storm, till we realized how they treat their fans," Jeremy said coolly, running his hand through his hair like he was in a music video. "Then we dropped them. Which is exactly what the rest of the world will do, too, once they hear Thunder and Lightning."

Jilly snorted.

"Wait till you hear our single," Cody told her, and when he looked straight at Jilly, I noticed her jaw go slack. Cody had killer eyes and a lifeguard vibe going for him. "We were given a song at the last minute, and it wound up being the one we recorded as our demo. That song got us a record deal with Perfect Storm's label."

"They're going down!" Jeremy lifted his hand, and Cody high-fived him.

My blood was beginning to boil. "Going down?"

Jilly grabbed my arm to hold me back. Mac Attack would know what to say in this situation. She'd sound smart and say something that put the boys in their place. "You…you…" They all stared at me. "You…" Why wouldn't the words come to me? "You wish!" I yelled as the screaming from the crowd intensified. Jeremy laughed at me. So much for channeling Mac Attack. "You'll never be as popular as Perfect Storm," I added.

Jeremy stopped laughing. His expression was stony. "We'll see about that. Come on, Cody." He motioned to his brother. "T and L out."

"T and L out?" Jilly called after them. "Who talks like that?"

I heard an announcement on someone's headset. "PS is on in five!"

"Did you just say T and L?" a man asked. He had a beach ball–size belly that was straining to stay covered under a white shirt. Three gold chains swung from his neck, one with the initial R. His black hair was slicked back with way too much hair product, and he smelled like Madam Celeste's tiny room, which made me start to hyperventilate. "Did you meet my boys? They're playing their hot new single during commercial breaks this morning, and they've only been on the Rock Starz label for two weeks. They're going to be HUGE! Do you want their autograph?"

"No," Jilly and I said at the same time. He blinked.

Perfect Storm's entourage was piling out of the greenroom to get the guys to the stage. Kyle,

Zander, and Heath were getting their earplugs and mics adjusted as they walked.

When Briggs saw Jilly, he looked at the man we were standing with and stopped short. "Ronald?"

"Briggsy! Good to see you, man." Ronald pumped Briggs's hand. "I'm here with my new band. They just signed to Rock Starz."

"Our label?" Kyle asked. "Brill. Where are the chaps?"

"Getting warmed up," Ronald said. "Thunder and Lightning killed this amazing ballad they nabbed for their demo. The girls are going to love them."

"I doubt it," I mumbled under my breath, and Mom looked at me.

"Boys, we have to move," Briggs said, and I could tell by his tone he didn't like Ronald or T and L much, either. "We have a show to do."

"Thunder and Lightning," Zander muttered. "That's a rip-off of our name!"

"Shake it off, mate." Kyle gave him a pat on the back. "Let's go wow them."

Wow them, they did. Even Raquel Rodgers seemed starstruck when Zander let her touch his curls (to the earsplitting screams of the audience). I stood at the side of the stage with Jilly, feeling proud, especially when Kyle looked over midsong and winked at me. There was nothing that could stop this summer from being the best one EVER.

Except what happened during the first commercial break.

LOCATION: My bedroom, which
I may never leave again!

Well, that was REALLY BAD.

Good Day USA should be renamed *Bad Day Go
Away.*

I'm sure it has nothing to do with Madam
Celeste's prediction. It's just a coincidence. A
really strange coincidence.

As PS grabbed water after their first set, Thunder and Lightning was heading onstage. Jeremy
and Cody shot daggers at PS as they passed.

"Get ready, PS," Jeremy said. "A storm is
coming!"

Zander's head whipped around. "That's our
line."

"That's T and L?" Heath sized up Jeremy and Cody as they took their mics. "We've got nothing to worry about."

"Hey, out there, I'm Jeremy," I heard him say in a smooth voice. The crowd of mostly girls started to scream at the top of their lungs even though they had no clue who he was. "Along with my younger brother, Cody, we are Thunder and Lightning, and we're here to make you fall in love with us."

Zander made a sound like he was choking.

"I love you already!" someone screamed.

"Some girls will crush on anyone with a microphone," I said to Jilly, who laughed. Which made me laugh—until I heard the first words of Thunder and Lightning's song. They sounded very familiar.

"*This is the story of a girl,*" Jeremy and Cody sang in unison while their guitars backed them up. "*See her standing there in her messed-up kicks, looking like she's got the whole world to fix...*"

"Mac," Jilly said worriedly. "Isn't that...?"

"That's our song!" Zander freaked out, the

color draining from his face. "Those rip-offs stole Kyle's song!" Kyle shushed him to listen.

Briggs and Mom came running over. "What's going on?" Mom said. She looked the way she usually does when my keys accidentally fall into the garbage disposal. (It's happened more than once.)

"With a smile that feels like a million watts and a laugh that makes me wanna rock," T and L continued to sing, and I knew for certain they were singing Kyle's song. But how?

Kyle's face twisted with each word till it looked more like a wrinkly pug than a cute boy bander. I felt my heart begin to flutter at an alarming rate. It seemed to be screaming,

The girls in the audience didn't know anything was wrong. They were going crazy; they were screaming so loud. Some girls were even crying, and others were throwing flowers onto the stage that I was certain were meant for PS. Traitors!

"They stole our song!" Heath said to Briggs. "How the heck did they get their hands on Kyle's lyrics?"

"I'm finding Ronald and getting answers." Briggs ran off.

"Oh! *She's a superhero in training, I'll be forever waiting,*" I heard T and L croon, and I cringed.

"Piper, do something!" Heath flipped. "People are recording this right now. They'll think this is their song!"

"There's nothing we can do till the song is over," Mom said. I noticed someone nearby pull out a camera phone and start recording the guys flipping out.

"Piper, this is rubbish! How could they get their hands on my song?" Kyle asked shakily. "You have to shut this down."

"Yeah!" I added angrily. "Pull the plug on those thieves!"

Heath and Zander looked at me, then at each other. I could see their minds working...

"No, mates, don't even think about it," Kyle started to say, but it was too late.

Just as my mother started to say "Mackenzie Sabrina Lowell," which was never a good sign, Zander and Heath dived for the plugs that ran from Thunder and Lightning's guitars to the speaker system. They yanked them out, and the music died. Zander and Heath high-fived as the *Good Day USA* crew scrambled to figure out what had happened.

I saw Jeremy's head snap to the side of the stage where we all stood. Cody nudged his brother to keep singing a cappella. *"This is the*

story of a girl, a girl who makes you want to whirl..." Jeremy snapped out of it and started singing again, too. "...a girl who makes you feel like you're miles from shore and you don't want for anything more. This is the story of a girl."

When the song ended, Jeremy and Cody picked up some flowers that had been thrown onstage and shook the hands of the girls within reach. Their smiles dropped the minute they got backstage. Jeremy came running at Heath, who barreled right back at him. I thought I was watching a wrestling match. The two boys collided in a war of words and hands, and the rest of us tried to pull them off each other. Mikey G., PS's bodyguard, muscled his way into the middle and separated both groups.

Cody and Ronald held Jeremy back. "You ruined our first live performance, you orange-haired freak!"

"Who are you calling a freak, you song-stealing hack!" Heath yelled as Jilly, Zander, Briggs, and I tried to hold him.

It was tough. He was really strong.

"You're just puppets with gelled hair," Jeremy yelled at him.

"My hair is naturally like this," Zander shouted, touching his hair to be sure it was as perfect as always. (It was. Even in the middle of a fight.)

"You probably perm it!" Cody shouted.

"Don't talk trash about my mates!" Kyle shoved him, and that's when I really began to worry.

Mom grabbed Jilly and me and pulled us out of the line of fire, but I could see people everywhere holding up phones and recording the fight.

"That's enough! Everyone in the greenroom now!" Briggs ordered, and the guys all stopped shouting and looked at each other. Heath's chest was rising and falling at an alarming rate.

Jeremy's cheeks looked red. We all filed off the side of the stage and into the greenroom, away from the prying eyes of cameras. When we were all there, Briggs looked at Ronald. "Where did you get that song your band just played?" he asked calmly.

Ronald scratched his head. "The boys came to me with it. I thought they wrote it. Didn't you?"

Jeremy folded his arms across his chest and stared at the ground. "No. A songwriter gave it to me personally."

"Then that songwriter stole it from us!" Heath said. "It's not yours!"

"Yes, it is," Cody huffed. "Rock Starz wants us to record it. Maybe it just sounds the same."

"Dude, it's the same lyrics!" Heath shouted. "You guys stole it!" Everyone started yelling again.

"Quiet!" Briggs said. "Ronald, there is no way someone wrote that song for them." Jeremy tried to interrupt, but Ronald shushed him. Briggs continued, "That song was written by Perfect Storm's Kyle Beyer. We're recording it as a single off Perfect Storm's next album."

"Rock Starz wants it to be *my* boys' first single," Ronald bragged. "They've hired a killer producer to rerecord the song with the guys next week so we can get it on their album."

"They can't record it," said an agitated Kyle. "I wrote that song, and you don't have my permission to use it."

"Well, this is a pickle," Ronald said, even though he was smiling. "Briggsy, you and I better go talk to the label. They're not going to want to pull this song from T and L. Especially not after they see the YouTube views for this." He held up his phone as proof. Someone had already uploaded T and L's performance of "The Story of a Girl."

"Let's go. Now," Briggs said to Ronald before glancing at Jeremy and Cody. "Do not perform that song again till you hear from our lawyers."

"You'll be hearing from our lawyers, too," Jeremy said smugly as he took a cup and dipped it into PS's Roaring Dragon fountain. "That song was given to us, and you can't take it."

"Yes, we can," said Heath, taking the cup from Jeremy. (He wasn't sharing *anything* today. Not even energy drinks.) "You've got a storm coming for you, and it's a big one."

Storm. A perfect storm. And I was right smack in the middle of it. Madam Celeste's words rang in my ears: "You have dark days ahead of you."

Thunder and Lightning left the greenroom,

and the *Good Day USA* crew rushed in to get the guys ready to go back on. I leaned against the wall, feeling exhausted.

"They totally stole Kyle's song about you," Jilly said, leaning her head on my shoulder. "This is a mess, but we can't just stand here." She grabbed my arm. "We've got to go cheer on the guys." She dragged me out of the room, then stopped short.

"Is that Lola Cummings?" Jilly pointed to an adjoining tent, where Jeremy was huddled with his arm around a blond girl in ripped jeans and a tank top. They were both watching something on the girl's cell phone, so I couldn't see her face.

"I don't think so," I said. "Why would she be with Jeremy?"

"You're right," Jilly said. "I'm just freaking out. Mac, this is bad. *Really* bad. How would someone have gotten their hands on Kyle's song?"

My heart started to beat faster. A tiny voice in the back of my head was pestering me, but I tried to ignore it. *I* had a copy of Kyle's song. He'd given it to me last spring in the hotel hallway right before I asked him to my school dance. But I never let my copy out of my sight. It was in my journal, which was always with me—*except* when I left it behind at SoundEscape.

"Kyle is the songwriter, and he never would have asked T and L to record it. He doesn't even

94

know them! He loves that song! He wrote it for you!" Jilly was saying almost to herself. "Someone had to steal it. But who?"

I was starting to break out in a cold sweat. Could someone have found my journal and ripped out the lyrics before Mom found it and gave it back to me?

My lips felt dry. I knew I should say something to Jilly, but I couldn't find the words. I pictured myself telling Iris and Scarlet my fears. Scarlet would yell at me like a drill sergeant, and Iris would cry that I'd ruined the boys' career. What would Jilly say? I didn't want to find out.

Jilly gasped, and her eyes widened. Could she read my mind? "Do you think that janitor at SoundEscape took the lyrics from the studio? Remember how he kept hanging outside the studio door waiting for the boys to sign a napkin?" She pulled out her phone. "I should call Dad and tell him to look into that guy."

I wasn't sure if the janitor was creepy or just an overexcited dad who had kids who liked PS, too. I didn't want the guy losing his job over a napkin. "Jilly, wait!" I said, and she stopped dialing. "I have to tell you something, and it's not good..."

Jilly looked at me. "What's wrong? You can tell me anything." She grabbed my hand.

I looked down at our wrists. We were wearing identical rainbow-colored rope knot bracelets. Iris, Scarlet, Jilly, and I had bought them in Stone Harbor together. Jilly had been so excited. "I've officially joined the Mac Attack band!" she'd joked, but it was true. Jilly was one of the Fab Four now. I trusted her like I trusted Iris and Scarlet. And in this case, she might be the only one who would understand. "About Kyle's lyrics," I started to say.

"You're right!" Jilly cut me off. "I'm probably jumping to conclusions. Chances are the only people who have a copy of Kyle's lyrics are in the band."

"They're not the only ones who have a copy," I said shakily. Then I took a deep breath and said the words that I dreaded saying aloud. "I have a copy, too. Taped in my journal that I lost for a minute that night Thunder and Lightning was also at the studio."

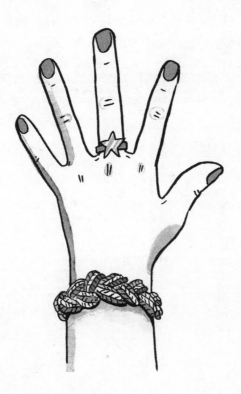

I'm so over Perfect Storm

Bad Kitty118

Subscribe

603,400

👍 200 👎 3000

Is Perfect Storm mean to their fans?
Bad Kitty here with the scoop! ME OW!

MORE

Thunder and Lightning.
Your new fave

bad kitty

bad cat

cat meowing

LOCATION: Beacon Theatre—New York City

I wish I had a helicopter like Mac Attack did in my comic book. I would have whisked Thunder and Lightning away before they started playing Kyle's song at *Good Day USA* last week.

If I had, some ridiculous vlogger, who calls herself Bad Kitty, wouldn't have grainy video footage of the PS and T and L fight backstage. Scarlet and Iris found her vlog when they were doing their daily PS search online. It's Bad Kitty's only post, but it already has thousands of views.

Bad Kitty wore big, black sunglasses that hid most of her face and a hoodie with cat ears that covered her hair. Her nose and cheeks were painted to look like she had whiskers, too.

"Hey, kitties!" the vlogger purred. "*Bad Kitty here, your new music guru, with a catfight alert! Is anyone else over Zander Welling, Heath Holland, and Kyle Beyer of Perfect Storm? I am!*" She raised her hand. "*They're never going to be huge when they don't treat their fans right. I've heard from numerous sources that the guys don't appreciate their followers. They actually ignore fans when they approach them on the street! Hiss!*" She clawed at the screen. "*Who needs that when new band Thunder and Lightning is the exact opposite?*" Bad Kitty was sitting in a dark room, so you couldn't see much around her, but she had a spotlight on a Thunder and Lightning poster. I couldn't believe those guys already had their own poster! "*These two sweet brothers—Jeremy and Cody Callum—had their first performance on Good Day USA last week, and their song, 'The Story of a Girl,' has gone viral! The guys have a record deal with Rock Starz, the same*

label as PS, and are heading out on the road soon. We hear PS is super jealous of the guys' song and is trying to get it pulled. Don't let it happen! Watch T and L's YouTube clip, and demand to be heard, cats!" Bad Kitty pawed at the screen with her super-long dark purple nails. "*You can also—*"

Scarlet clicked off the video. "It's not their song! This is why I hate cats. They're mean!"

"Shouldn't a vlogger know the facts before she posts videos?" Iris was angry, too. "She should be fired from her own vlog!"

"I don't think that's going to happen." Jilly pried the tablet from Iris's hands, which wasn't easy to do. All those years of tae kwon do have made her really strong. "You can't get caught up in what one blogger says anyway," she told us, sounding a lot like a mini version of her dad. "No one will pay any attention to some silly girl in a cat hoodie."

But the media *did* pay attention. Bad Kitty's video began popping up on entertainment shows and music blogs. It even had a link on CNN's website. ("I told you this would happen!" Scarlet freaked out. "You need to call Nicole, Ryan, and Stanley T. at The Morning Mash Up on SiriusXM immediately!" Iris added. "They can tell the world PS's side of the story.") But Briggs didn't listen to my friends. Within days, everyone was talking about Thunder and Lightning's song "The Story of a Girl." And the worst part was, Rock Starz wanted to keep the truth about the tune being Kyle's quiet! Briggs and Ronald met with the label to hash out an agreement, and Briggs was not happy with the results. I'm not sure of all the legal lingo—I yawn when my grandparents watch Law & Order—but I do know that Kyle gets songwriting credit on "The Story of a Girl." Yay! But it's Thunder and Lightning's version that will be released, since it already went viral. Boo! The guys have been in such foul moods I haven't talked to Kyle in days (although I did text him a picture I drew of PS in superhero costumes, and he texted back a happy-face emoji).

And things were still going from bad to worse.

"What do you think of the name 'Sizzling Summer Boys Tour'?" Mom asked one night while I was working on my comic. She made a bizarre face that I associate with bad news. "It's the name of the Perfect Storm–slash–Thunder and Lightning tour."

"WHAT?" I Hulked out, slamming the table so hard my sketchbook slid off. "They can't go on tour together!"

"It's not ideal, but Briggs and I don't know what else to do," Mom said grimly. "The label thinks a ten-city East Coast tour will benefit both bands." I opened my mouth to argue. "The media coverage has upped the profile of each group. Now the label wants them to make nice on tour and stop taking swipes at each other in the press."

"But they can't stand each other," I reminded Mom. "They're going to get into fights, the media is going to report it, the guys are going to be miserable, and..." This tour did not sound fun. I couldn't picture Kyle laughing with me on the bus, or Heath shooting spitballs at Briggs, or Jilly and me facing off against the guys at a game of mini golf. Not with the boys in their current mood. I was about to say all that when I stopped short.

Had I lost my mind? Was I really about to suggest we NOT go on the road with my favorite

band in the world? The guys NEEDED me now more than ever! I could be their lighthouse in the storm on this tour. (Oooh! That was a great idea for a new PS tee. A lighthouse guiding a ship through a major storm. I needed to get on that.)

Mom hugged me. "I know with you on the road with them, Perfect Storm will cheer up in no time." She looked at me. "This is going to be a challenging tour. I'm counting on you to be a mini tour manager for me."

"I get a title?" I pictured my new pass: ASSISTANT TOUR MANAGER MACKENZIE S. LOWELL. Pink glitter paint would make those words pop.

Mom laughed. "Well, unofficially, but I mean it. I need you to be my eyes and ears on the road. Don't let Thunder and Lightning get to Perfect Storm."

"I can do that," I said, saluting Mom for added effect.

"Then I can handle catching up on this week's episodes of *Life After Life* and ordering in takeout from La Piazza for dinner," Mom said.

Things were starting to look up.

Or so I thought. Darn Madam Celeste!

When Jeremy and Cody Callum showed up for our first Sizzling Summer Boys Tour appearance at the Beacon Theatre in New York, Lola Cummings was with them.

"Aww, look! If it isn't the Perfect Storm fan club." Lola walked toward us in heels so high I thought they were stilts. Her cheetah print pants clashed in a cool way against her leopard print top.

"I guess Perfect Storm fans are dropping like flies now that the world knows how they treat their fans," Jeremy sneered. "You two are the only ones they seem to have left."

Jilly folded her arms across her chest and glared at T and L. Jilly was five feet of pure fury. Cody seemed a tad scared of her. "The only reason there aren't fans here right now is because

111

there is no meet and greet backstage tonight. With all these lies about PS out there, everyone backstage needs to sign a confidentiality agreement now. We don't want anything else of PS's *stolen*." She looked pointedly at Jeremy.

"Who would want those losers' leftovers?" Jeremy asked. Jilly lunged at him.

Mikey G. appeared. "Problem?" He would have looked menacing if he wasn't in the middle of eating one of his beloved WHEY OUT! protein bars. I thought WHEY OUT! smelled like glue. Mikey G. once offered me a piece of one, and it tasted like glue, too.

"She didn't sign a confidentiality agreement." Jilly pointed to Lola, who began to protest when

Mikey G. gently took her by the arm. Jeremy didn't protest when he saw Mikey G. charging Lola's way.

"I'm not signing a confidentiality agreement!" she said stiffly, and that's all Mikey G. had to hear before he led her out a side door and onto an Upper West Side sidewalk.

In the middle of the commotion, I saw Cody turn to Jilly. "Cool kicks," he said quietly. I looked down at Jilly's sneakers—one was pink and the other was white. They both had sparkly silver laces.

"Meep!" Jilly sounded like an alien. "I mean, you're not allowed to like my shoes!" Then Jilly started coughing so hard I thought she was going to throw up. Cody walked away, and Mikey G. raised an eyebrow at me.

"Are you okay?" I asked her.

"I must be allergic to Cody's cologne," Jilly said.

"Or to Cody," Mikey G. joked, and we both laughed.

"Did you fill out a confidentiality agreement?" she asked me stormily. We stopped laughing. "Everyone needs one. I already did mine."

I was the tour manager's daughter. Why would I need a confidentiality agreement? "Ummm..." Mikey G. was staring at me like he had Lola. "I'll do it now. I would never do anything to hurt PS."

I imagined myself in a courtroom signing the agreement in front of Perfect Storm and onlookers. An image of my journal lying in the recording studio flashed through my head. "At least not on purpose," I added.

"What does that mean?" Mikey G. asked darkly.

"I think you need to tell Mikey G. what happened—or didn't happen," Jilly said. I protested. "Maybe he can help you keep it from happening—or not happening—again."

114

Mikey G. took another bite of his bar. "I'm very confused."

Jilly was right. Mikey G. was the best body-guard I knew. Well, he was the only bodyguard I knew, but still! Maybe if I let him look after my journal when I wasn't writing in it, I wouldn't have to worry about anyone getting their hands on it again. *If* someone even got their hands on it in the first place, and…Oh, this was so confusing! I looked around the crowded area. Mom hurried by, calling out orders. People were shouting for equipment and craft services spreads. I couldn't talk about this here. I pulled Jilly and Mikey G. out the side door he'd just pushed Lola through.

"If I tell you something, you have to swear on your love of all things PS that you will never breathe a word of this to another soul," I said.

Mikey G. exhaled sharply. "You didn't write another one of those poems asking the guys to a dance, did you?"

Once again my face felt like it was boiling.

"How did you...NO! I did not write anyone a letter." Jilly tried not to laugh.

Mikey G. took another bite of his WHEY OUT! bar. "Spill."

Better to just blurt it out and get it over with. "I may have accidentally left my journal with Kyle's lyrics for 'The Story of a Girl' in the recording studio."

"YOU DID WHAT?" Mikey G. yelled. People walking by on the street gave us nervous glances.

"No one took it," Jilly said quickly. "We don't *think*." Mikey G. raised an eyebrow. "Mac's mom found the journal when she went back to grab something later."

"At least *someone* was thinking," Mikey G. said.

My eyes narrowed. "That horrible moment made me realize how valuable my journal is. I write in it almost every day about everything that happens on the road. If it fell into the wrong hands, people would know all kinds of secrets about the guys."

"Maybe the best thing to do is to stop writing in your journal," Jilly suggested.

"Stop writing?" I repeated in shock.

"She's an artist," Mikey G. explained to Jilly. "She lives to create."

I felt myself get a little misty. Mikey G. got me. "Thanks. I always thought—"

He cut me off. "But it's dumb to carry something that valuable around. If you were to lose it, it could be a disaster."

"I know," I said with a sigh. "What am I going to do?"

"Let me hold on to it," he said, taking it from

my hands before I had time to react. "When you want to write in it, I'll give it to you."

"Okay." I looked longingly at the journal in Mikey G.'s hands. I was a little nervous knowing I wouldn't always have it at my fingertips. What if Mikey G. read it? What if he left it out and Kyle read it? Or Heath? I'd never live it down! "But don't read it," I blurted out. "It's private."

"I know," Mikey G. deadpanned. "I have no interest in reading it, and I don't want anyone else reading it, either. That's why I'm hiding it in my *Life After Life* DVD case." He sized up my journal with his beefy hands. "No one will look in that thing."

"That's for sure," Jilly said with a snort, and Mikey G. and I glared at her. "I mean, I like the show, but it's not my favorite. Geez."

As Kyle would say, Mikey G.'s hiding place was "brill." "Thanks, Mikey G."

His serious expression turned into a slow smile. Then he fist-bumped me. "Don't worry. I'd do anything for the boys and you. I've got your back."

Mikey G. may have had my back, but Mom seemed to think I did *not* have Perfect Storm's tonight. I'm still fuming about the fight we just had. It ended with us slamming doors and not saying good night. And we always say good night!

Now I'm too wound up to fall asleep. Thank God Mikey G. gave me my journal back to write in. ("But you just put it in my trust!" he complained as he took it out of the *Life After Life* case and handed it to me backstage. I swore I'd have it back to him when we got on the tour bus tomorrow morning.)

We're heading out on the Sizzling Summer Boys Tour tomorrow, and I haven't even packed yet. That's how mad I am. I could pinkie-swear Jeremy Callum screwed up tonight's tour kickoff concert on purpose.

Here's what happened: *Obviously* Perfect Storm is the bigger act, so Briggs said management agreed Thunder and Lightning would be the opener. They hoped the groups would do an encore performance together. But that seemed unlikely even *before* tonight's disastrous performance.

After Jilly and I gave Mikey G. my journal, we headed backstage again, where Jeremy was throwing a rock star tantrum.

"Why does their set get to be longer than ours?" he bickered with Ronald. "This is a joint tour, and Perfect Storm is trying to hog the whole show!"

Jilly and I dived behind a giant speaker to hear more. I could see Jeremy perfectly. He had his guitar slung over his shoulder, and he was wearing a plain white tee and ripped jeans. It was very much an *I'm too cool to care what I wear* look, and I hated it. Cody had at least put in the effort with a black jacket, black jeans, and Converse.

"Jeremy," Ronald said patiently, "you guys are the openers. You only have one single, and we had to fight to even keep that one. Take the gig and run with it."

"I want six songs, not three," Jeremy pouted.

"What a baby," Jilly whispered to me.

"Maybe Ronald's right," Cody tried. "Let's nail the three songs we've got and leave the stage with the fans wanting more."

"They already *do* want more," Jeremy said, and held out his phone as proof. "Look at this video Lola sent me of girls singing our song." He pressed play, and I heard girls singing "The Story of a Girl."

I wanted to scream. That was my song!

"Our Twitter followers doubled this week, and I'm sure it's thanks to that Bad Kitty vlogger. People love T and L, and with Bad Kitty telling them how jealous Perfect Storm is of us, their days are numbered."

That was it! I began to march out from my hiding place, but Jilly held me back.

"They're not worth it," she whispered. "At least Jeremy isn't."

"Thunder and Lightning on in five!" a roadie announced.

"You guys have to get out there," Ronald said. "Make nice, stick to a fifteen-minute set, and we'll ask for more time on the next stop. Okay?"

Jeremy didn't answer, but Cody nodded. "Sounds good, Ron. Thank you." He put an arm around his brooding brother, and they headed to the stage just as Heath flew by on his skateboard. He came to a stop right in front of Jilly and me.

"Spying on the enemy?" he asked with a grin.

"No," I said, but I'm a terrible liar. My nose starts to twitch, and I begin to sneeze. It's not attractive. "We were just— ACHOO!"

"Gesundheit!" Heath said. "And you're lying. Just admit it. What did they say?"

"They want more time onstage," Jilly said. "Jeremy was complaining that you guys are the headliners."

Heath looked to the side of the stage where Jeremy and Cody had disappeared. "I hate that we're going on the road with them."

"It's only for nine more shows," I said. I had to keep reminding myself of that, too. I liked having PS all to myself on tour. I also liked not worrying every second of the day that someone was trying to steal my journal to ruin PS's reputation.

"That's more than half the summer," Heath pointed out. "I can't even— OUCH!"

A foam pellet hit him in the side of the head, and I heard giggling.

"Get out of here, rats," Heath called. I saw his mischievous twin brothers, Tristan and Isaac, appear from behind a vending machine and a light-up PS sign that wasn't being used tonight. I'd forgotten his little brothers had flown into New York for tonight's kickoff show. "Briggsy will kill me if he knows you have those things backstage."

"You gave them to us," Tristan said. Or maybe it was Isaac. They were identical, and their shaggy brown hair would have matched Heath's if his wasn't dyed bright blue today.

"You said to aim at those guys." The other twin pointed to Jeremy and Cody.

"Yes, and instead you're aiming at me." Heath whipped out a mini toy blaster. The three of them ran around in circles hitting each other with foam pellets while Jilly and I watched from outside the line of fire.

Zander stormed out of a dressing room with Kyle on his tail. "Would you guys keep it down?"

Kyle gave a little wave. I shyly waved back. We hadn't had a lot of time to talk since his song was stolen. I felt like I should say something to him like "It wasn't me! At least I *think* it wasn't. Not on purpose!" But no matter how many times I rehearsed it, I couldn't say the words.

"Kyle and I are trying to write an epic new single, and all this yelling is distracting us," Zander fumed. One of the twins responded by hitting him in the chest with a foam arrow. "We don't have time for games."

"Sorry," I said, looking directly at Kyle. Because I was. The last thing I'd ever want is to screw up things for him and the band. "We'll keep it down."

Jilly was less diplomatic. "You guys need to chill," she said, taking a spin on Heath's skateboard. "Aren't you going on soon, anyway?"

I could faintly hear cheering from the audience, so I knew T and L's set was still going. I looked at my watch. Huh? They'd gone way over their time limit already!

"We should be." Zander frowned and walked over to the side of the stage. We all followed, including Heath's brothers and Mikey G. That's where we saw Briggs and my mom arguing with Ronald. Briggs and Mom walked away in a huff.

"I'm sorry, boys," Mom told the guys when she saw us. "They were supposed to be off the stage ten minutes ago so that we can reset, but they keep playing all these cover songs!"

Jilly and I peeked around the curtain. Jeremy and Cody were running around the stage with their guitars, singing in unison. Annoyingly, they sounded pretty good, and the crowd was eating them up. "Want another one?" I heard Jeremy say when the cover they were singing ended. The crowd screamed their approval, and I spotted Lola Cummings, her bestie, and her babysitter in the front row. Lola held up her phone, recording the concert. I felt like steam was escaping out of my ears.

"They can't do that," Heath huffed. "We're supposed to go on by nine, and we haven't even set up yet. You have to pull them."

"I'm trying!" Briggs sounded agitated. "Ronald can't get their attention."

"There are all these bloggers out there," Mom added. "We don't want to cause a scene." Mom looked at me as if to say *Help me.* But help her how? I felt my pocket vibrate, and I pulled out my phone. Scarlet was group-texting me and Iris. Neither of them could make tonight's show because they had the junior chorus concert (Mrs. Southers didn't take too kindly to them asking to skip the concert to see PS).

SCARLET'S CELL: OMG, are T and L really still onstage? Bad Kitty is tweeting that the guys are so hot, no one wants PS to come on!!!!

IRIS'S CELL: T and L can't cut into PS time! Why isn't your mom doing something!!!??? PULL THEM OFFSTAGE!

"This is rubbish," Kyle said. "They'll never leave if we don't make them."

"I'll have the lighting crew dim the stage or cut their mics," Mom said, and gave us all a pointed look before rushing off. "Don't do anything rash."

I think that last remark was meant for me. I was a little insulted. When was I ever rash?

Zander groaned and held up his phone. "Did you guys see these tweets? Bad Kitty says: 'Who wants PS when T and L are killing it? Hashtag PSGoHome.'"

"We have to do something," Heath agreed.

Jeremy was playing his guitar close to our side of the stage. He winked at Heath. "Who wants to hear our hot single, 'The Story of a Girl'?" Jeremy asked, and the crowd went wild as they began to play.

"Why, that little…" Zander ran for Jeremy, and Kyle held him back.

"He's not worth it, mate," Kyle said.

131

"Heath!" one of his twin brothers whined as I listened to the words I knew by heart. They didn't sound the same with Jeremy and Cody singing them. "Let's play more."

"Later, buddy," Heath said. His eyes were locked on the stage, where Cody was now heavy into a solo. "First, I have to deal with these guys. I can't stand hearing them sing our song."

"I'll get 'em!" the other twin said, and before anyone could stop him, he took aim at Cody. A pellet whizzed past us and hit Cody in the back of the

leg. No one in the audience seemed to notice, but Zander and Heath did. They looked at each other.

"Guys," I heard Kyle say warningly.

"It would get them off the stage," Zander said to Heath.

"It's not like it's going to hurt them," Heath added.

"Piper said she'd take care of this," Kyle tried as Heath took a blaster from one of the twins. Zander grabbed the other one.

"Ready, aim, fire!" Heath aimed at Jeremy's guitar. Zander did the same.

The pellets hit Jeremy's cheek and his guitar. He stopped singing for a second and turned toward our side of the stage to see what was going on. That's when Heath shot a pellet right into his open mouth. "YES!" Heath high-fived his brothers.

Jeremy came storming toward us and shut off his mic. "What do you think you're doing?"

"Getting you off *our* stage," Zander said.

Jeremy held out an ear to the audience. "Do you hear that? They're chanting our name, not yours. I don't think anyone wants us off that stage. We're not leaving."

"Get off now." Heath shot another pellet at Cody, who was looking bewilderingly offstage.

"Make me." Jeremy stole the blaster from Zander and headed back out with it. He aimed at us.

"Incoming!" Jilly said, and we all dived for cover.

Heath fired back and looked at his brothers. "What else do you guys have with you tonight?"

"We have those bows and arrows Mom says will cause an eye injury," one of the twins said hopefully.

"And two *Star Wars* blasters that shoot Silly String," the other twin added.

"Get them!" Heath said. "And fast."

The twins were back quickly, and within minutes we all had something. At least T and L wasn't singing at this point. The band tried

134

to keep going for a few minutes, but eventually they took cover. Jeremy slipped on an arrow and tripped, which made Heath roar as he rushed the stage. Soon the guys were chasing each other around in front of the audience. Jilly and I were cracking up.

Until we heard Mom.

"WHAT IS GOING ON?" Mom bellowed as an arrow whizzed past her ear. "Mackenzie Sabrina Lowell, I told you to keep an eye on them!"

"She did," Jilly replied. "She hasn't taken her eyes off them—while they battle."

Mom's walkie-talkie was going mad. I could hear different people yelling about the destruction of the set and the mess the boys were making. Heath pulled down a Thunder and Lightning sign, and Jeremy grabbed a PS prop from the other side of the stage and threw it into the audience. The audience seemed to think this was all part of the show, because they were still cheering wildly. (Louder, I might add, since PS got out there.) Things were quickly getting out of hand.

"Jillian Michelle, this is not funny!" Briggs said, running over a few seconds later. He got on one of the walkie-talkies. "Shut the show down. I don't know for how long. Just shut it!"

"You're shutting down the show?" I was flabbergasted. "PS didn't go on yet!"

"Now they may not get to," Briggs said grimly. "I better talk to the theater managers and try to salvage this. Otherwise, we will have witnessed our first Thunder and Lightning solo performance."

That is the last thing I wanted. "We'll make them stop," I pleaded.

But it was too late. The house lights came on, and then a voice came over the loudspeaker system. "Ladies and gentlemen, please excuse this interruption. The Sizzling Summer Boys Show has been temporarily halted. Please stay in your seats and..." I heard the audience groan. I looked at my mom and saw her Deeply Disappointed face.

"I can't believe you egged them on," Mom said. "Why didn't you try to stop them? I was counting on you to help me, Mac."

"The guys couldn't be stopped!" I protested. Deep down, I knew the truth: I did nothing to help Perfect Storm avoid the mayhem, either.

Mom and I continued arguing all night. All through PS's shortened set. All through Mom's yelling at the boys backstage, and the whole way home to Long Island.

A little while later, I heard a soft knock on my door and sat up in time to see my door open and a hand waving a white napkin. "Hold all foam pellet fire. I come in peace."

I couldn't help but giggle. "It's safe. You can come in."

Mom walked in. She had on her favorite

pajamas—a tank top with a gorilla playing drums and bottoms with a zillion guitars on them. I pulled back my covers and pointed to my tank top. We were wearing the same pj's! We'd bought them in Atlanta this past spring.

"Well, that says it all, doesn't it?" Mom sat on

the edge of my bed. "We go to bed mad, but we still put on the same pj's. We think a lot alike. I'm hoping that means you know what I'm thinking right now."

I tried to channel Madam Celeste, but nothing came to me. Darn it.

"I'm sorry, Mac," Mom said, opening her arms wide for a hug. I didn't have to be asked twice. I practically jumped out of my comforter and landed in her arms. "What happened tonight wasn't your fault. It was mine." I looked at her. "I shouldn't have left the side of the stage when I saw what was happening with T and L. I should have known the boys would go crazy."

"I still should have told them to stop instead of cheering them on," I admitted. "That stupid battle almost cost them the concert."

"It all worked out in the end." She sighed. "I just hope we don't go through this at every concert."

I hoped not, too. "Am I stripped of my assistant tour manager duties?" I asked.

"No. It means I have to do a better job as *main* tour manager." Mom pulled away and held out her pinkie. "Let's make a deal. I'll be better at my job if you'll be better at yours." I looked at her. "Your job is to be a good friend to the guys. If PS is acting crazy, tell them. Don't egg them on. If they don't listen, come find me. Deal?"

I linked my pinkie with hers and smiled. "You've got a deal."

Tuesday, June 21

LOCATION: Love Park—Philadelphia, Pennsylvania

PS was shooting a music video today, and Mom, Mikey G., and Briggs were with them. Jilly was off doing who-knows-what, so I had the tour bus all to myself this morning. I was eating cereal, enjoying the quiet, when I felt a tap on my shoulder. I switched into Mac Attack mode, jumping, then spinning around to take down my intruder with a well-placed roundhouse kick. I quickly realized I was about to pummel Kyle.

"I surrender!" He held up his hands. He looked cute in a white Henley, rolled jeans, and white high-tops.

"Sorry!" I had almost kicked my favorite boy

bander in the gut! I could just imagine Bad Kitty's next vlog post—KYLE BEYER INJURED! SIZZLING SUMMER BOYS TOUR NOW FEATURES THUNDER AND LIGHTNING ONLY! YAY!

"Blimey. Who'd you think I was?" Kyle asked.

Bad Kitty? Jeremy and Cody Callum? Madam Celeste here to deliver more bad news? The Sharkinator? I wasn't sure. All I knew was that I was anxious. Bad Kitty and other bloggers were having a field day with the story about last weekend's concert at the Beacon (PERFECT STORM TRIES TO SABOTAGE THUNDER AND LIGHTNING'S SET! Bad Kitty posted. I wanted to claw her eyes out). "I watched a scary movie with Jilly last night, and I'm still a little jumpy."

I watched Kyle run a hand through his short hair as if it were happening in slow motion. "Right. Well, if there are any ghosts around, I'll protect you."

Aww...Kyle was so cute! "Thanks."

"I have some brilliant news that should take your mind off ghosts," Kyle said.

"Thunder and Lightning is leaving the tour?" I asked hopefully. Kyle shook his head. "You've written an even better single than 'The Story of a Girl'?"

Kyle laughed. "You are aces, Mackenzie Lowell, but no."

I'd never heard Kyle call me by my full name before. When Mom said it, it meant I was in serious trouble. But when Kyle said it, it sounded really nice.

"I'd like to be done with a new song in time for it to go on the album, but I need that spark of inspiration to kick me off," he explained. "You know, like you with your comics or your journal. What do you write about?"

Um, you? But I didn't say that. "Whatever is going on in my life. I love spilling my guts to a piece of paper."

"I'll have to try that one of these days when we aren't about to shoot a video for twelve hours," Kyle said. "But that's not the surprise." His eyes were extra sparkly in the morning light.

145

"Guess who gets to be an extra in our video today?"

If it was possible for my heart to stop and then start again quickly, that is exactly what happened. "ME?" I screamed. Kyle nodded. "I'm going to be in the 'Just Another Love Song' video?" He nodded again.

I jumped up and hugged him. I was touching Kyle Beyer. I had my arms around Kyle Beyer. Wow, he smelled nice. I quickly pulled away. "What do I need to do?" I asked, trying to sound serious and not at all interested in the fact that Kyle smelled like maple syrup.

"I knew you'd be excited!" Kyle laughed. "First, we have to get you to hair and makeup. They have the trailer set up a ways down the road. I'll show you where."

I grabbed my journal and decided I'd give it to Mikey G. on the way to hair and makeup. I was pretty sure he'd be there—Mikey G. made a cameo in all the guys' videos.

146

Kyle led the way as I quickly sent Scarlet, Iris, and Jilly a group text. We had started doing more and more of those since Iris and Scarlet named themselves PS Social Media Command Central and started sending us links to crazy blog posts and Bad Kitty vlogs. IM GONNA BE IN NEW PS VIDEO! I tried to type, but my hands were shaking so bad, I wound up writing: IM GONNA BE IN PS NEVER VITAL! Darn autocorrect.

IRIS'S CELL: What's a never vital?

SCARLET'S CELL: WHAT??? Did someone call them not vital? WHO?

JILLY'S CELL: She means new video. I'm in it 2! Get 2 makeup, Mac!

ME: New video!!! Will send deets soon! And pics!

I put my phone on vibrate as the girls started to text me like crazy. I wondered what Jilly and I would be doing in the video. Was Kyle going to be singing to me? I wasn't sure I could stand it if he was. Girls fainted at PS shows all the time. I practiced breathing in and out and staying Zen. Wasn't that what Mom did with yoga? I exhaled slowly. Okay, that felt good. I was going to ooze calmness. Mac Attack was always relaxed, whether she was hanging from a helicopter by a string or talking to the president. If I could be calm in a PS video, maybe they would start putting me in ALL their videos! I could be their video girl! People would see me at concerts and say, "It's the girl from the PS videos." And then I would sign autographs and take selfies like a good celebrity should. Then maybe I'd get so popular someone from the Totally TV network would call and ask if I wanted to guest-star on one of their shows. I'd be on *Alex and Abby* as their wacky new school friend. The episode would be such a huge hit that Totally TV would ask if I wanted my own show! Then I would pitch

with love,
~~with love,~~
Mackenzie Lowell
Mackenzie Lowell
Mackenzie Lowell
~~✗~~
Mackenzie Lowell ♡

Mac Attack for TV and sign a multimillion-dollar contract and…

"Mac? Did you hear me?" Kyle was waving a hand in front of my face.

My TV fantasy went POOF! "Sorry! I was just getting into character for the video." I cleared my throat. What did people do to warm up their voice? Say their ABCs? I decided to give it a shot. I was at the letter G before Kyle put a hand on my arm.

"I don't think you have any lines," he said

with a lopsided smile that made me drool. "There's usually no talking in these bits. Just us singing, or pretending to. But I'm sure you'll be brill no matter what they have you do." We smiled goofily at each other. Then Jilly ran up and tackled me.

"Can you believe we get to be in a video?" she exclaimed.

She'd obviously had her hair blown out, because instead of her usual bun, her hair was sleek with shimmery sparkles in it. She was also wearing a Perfect Storm glitter tee, which she wouldn't be caught dead in under normal circumstances.

"And at Love Park, too, which is the perfect place to shoot the 'Just Another Love Song' video," Jilly jabbered on. "It's just a bummer they banned skateboarding, because it's the perfect place for it." We stared at the bubbling fountain and the smooth cement surrounding the red sculpture that spelled out the word "LOVE."

"We can skateboard here today," Kyle told her. "Briggs got permission for the video shoot. Look! The professionals are already warming up." He nodded to where a few skateboarders who looked a lot like Heath were doing crazy tricks and flips. Maybe they were Heath's stunt doubles.

"Sweet!" Jilly smiled, and the glittery PS tattoo on her cheek seemed to jump. Her smile faded when she looked down at my right hand. "You brought your journal to the video shoot?" She gave me a pointed glance.

My journal! I had to get this to Mikey G. "Oh, I guess I'll just have Mikey G. bring it back to the bus for me. Have you seen him?"

"He's in the makeup trailer," Jilly said. "I'd give it to him right away, so he can put it back before you both start filming. I would do it for you, but I want to see if they'll let me skateboard, too, and practice some tricks."

Was there anything Jilly couldn't do?

"And I have to do a run-through with the guys," Kyle said. "So now that I've escorted you safely to the makeup trailer without any ghost sightings, I'll leave you. Ask for Phyllis in the trailer. She's the best." He winked at me before walking away.

I ran up the metal steps to the makeup trailer, which looked a lot like our tour bus. Inside, though, everything was different. All the furniture had been removed, and makeup stations and lighted mirrors had taken their place. Someone was setting a wig, another artist was blow-drying a girl's hair, and a third was doing a haircut.

wink

"Can I help you?" said one of the hairstylists.

"I'm looking for Phyllis," I said. "I'm an extra in the video."

"I'm Phyllis!" said a big blond woman with curly hair. She was wearing a loose tee that had LONG LIVE ROCK written in glitter. "I'll be right with you, hon. Just finishing up Jeremy's cut."

Jeremy?

I walked around the makeup chair to get a closer look, and there was Jeremy Callum, humming "The Story of a Girl" while Phyllis cut his hair!

"You're not supposed to be in here." My voice sounded shrill. "This isn't your video!"

Phyllis stopped cutting and looked at me oddly. Did she even know who was in Perfect Storm and who wasn't?

"Relax, kid," Jeremy said to me.

Kid? I was not a kid!

"My group opens for Perfect Storm, at least for now, so I'm stuck here while we wait for our

153

hotel rooms to be ready. The least PS can do is buy me a haircut." Jeremy looked at me, his brown eyes blazing. "Like I'd want to be in their video. I'm just hanging with Phyllis here because she's got the magic touch."

"Jeremy, you are too sweet," Phyllis said, totally falling for Jeremy's lines. "Let me get some of that awesome hair balm for you to try, and then we'll get you on your way. You're going to send me that single of yours when it's done, right?"

"Phyllis, I'm going to send a case for you and everyone at Technique Professionals," Jeremy told her with a smile. As soon as she disappeared, his trademark scowl returned.

"You are such a fake!" I hissed in his ear. I had to get that close to him to be heard over the whir of the blow-dryers. "You won't even remember her name tomorrow!"

"So?" Jeremy shrugged.

154

"It's not even your song to begin with! You stole it!" I freaked out.

He laughed. "It's mine now. That's all that matters."

"All you want to do is mess with PS. I swear, if you do anything to ruin this video shoot for them, I will…I will…" What would Mac Attack do to someone like Jeremy? I looked at the scissors Phyllis left on the table. Jeremy saw me staring at them and grabbed them.

"Don't get any ideas," he said. Then he got out of the chair and gelled a piece of his dark hair back while staring in the mirror. "Messing up my hair won't keep us from crushing PS on the charts."

Without thinking, I tried to hit him in the head with my journal. Jeremy saw it coming and grabbed it.

"What's this?" he asked. OH NO. OH NO. OH NO! He held my journal over his head.

"Give it back!" I jumped for it.

155

"Give the girl her stuff. NOW." Mikey G. was standing behind us, looking super styled with spiky hair and what looked like blush on his cheeks.

"Whatever." Jeremy tossed me the book. "Like I'd want to read your journal. You're not worth my time. I have bigger fish to fry than some PS groupie." Jeremy pushed past me.

"Groupie? I am not a groupie! I am a super fan, and you're messing with my favorite band. You won't get away with it!" I yelled as the blow-dryer near me seemed to get louder. I handed Mikey G. the journal.

"Don't walk around with this thing," Mikey G. scolded me. "I'll put it back. Then I have to get to my scene."

Phyllis appeared with an armful of hair gels. "Where's Jeremy?"

"Jeremy?" I heard Heath say as he and the guys shut the makeup trailer door behind them. They high-fived Mikey G. as they passed him on his way out. "What was that dude doing in here? Were you talking to that guy?" Heath asked me, sounding annoyed.

"He was talking to me," I clarified. Because it was mostly true.

"He and his brother are the enemy. They should not be talking to our girl," Heath said. "Phyllis! I'm ready for my wash and go!" He bounded off to an empty chair.

Phyllis laughed. "Let's get all of you washed so we can get you out there."

I liked that Heath called me "our girl," but the way Zander and Kyle were looking at me had me worried that I might not be their girl for long.

"Did he ask you what we were recording?" Zander pressed. "Did Jeremy ask how I was doing my hair? That dude is seriously trying to copy my look. Phyllis! Give me something new today, okay?" He headed to the shampoo chair.

"What did Jeremy want to talk to you about?"

Kyle asked. His voice wasn't as friendly as it was earlier.

"It was nothing." I didn't want Kyle to know Jeremy had called me a kid.

"Steer clear of those guys." Kyle still wasn't smiling. "They're trouble."

"Kyle! Time to wash that gorgeous hair of yours!" Phyllis called, and Kyle walked away without saying good-bye. Humph! "Sweet pea, you stay put," she added. "I'll do your makeup in a few."

I sat down in the nearest chair and watched all three boys get their hair shampooed. I'd barely taken my phone out to text Jilly and the girls about what just happened when I heard Phyllis scream.

"What is wrong with this shampoo!" she said, turning to the other stylists. "It's bleaching their hair!"

"Bleach?" Zander whimpered, sitting up fast and sending water flying everywhere. "WAIT! Why do I have orange hair?"

Heath sat up and ran a towel through his hair to dry off. He looked in the mirror next to him and saw his hair—which had already been orange—was now platinum blond. "Cool. I was going to dye my hair this shade next anyway."

"Where did this bleach come from?" One of the stylists held up a squirt bottle. "This was for Lemon Ade's dye job tomorrow. What's it doing next to the shampoo?"

"The hair products have been compromised!" Zander jumped up and stole Heath's mirror. He began to whimper when he saw his reflection. "My hair! I look like a clown. Someone do something! We have a video shoot today!"

One of the stylists looked nervously from Zander to Phyllis. "If we tried to dye it back, it would just make things worse. We need to wait twenty-four hours."

"WHAT?" Zander was seriously bugging out.

"Sweetie, it doesn't look that bad!" Phyllis tried, but Zander was beside himself.

"Jeremy did this!" Kyle shouted. "He was in here talking to Mac."

"I thought that darling Jeremy was laying it on a bit thick," Phyllis declared. "I should have known he was up to no good."

"Mac, you know Jeremy is jealous of my hair!" Zander whined.

"Dude, your hair looks cool," Heath said,

smiling at himself in the mirror Zander was still holding. "Embrace being orange for one day."

"We have a video shoot!" Zander reminded him. "Do you know what our fans will think if they see me like this? I hope I don't lose Twitter followers." Zander looked at me. "Mac, how could you let this happen?"

"This isn't my fault!" I felt myself get misty. How could I go from being their girl to PS Enemy Number One in minutes? "I told Jeremy to leave!"

Briggs walked into the makeup trailer, saw PS, and groaned. "What happened?"

"Jeremy sabotaged our shampoo," Kyle said, and he glanced my way again.

"Did any of you *see* Jeremy tamper with the bottles?" Briggs asked wearily.

"No, but Mac might have," Heath said, and all eyes were on me again.

"I didn't," I said guiltily. I was letting the guys down. Again.

"This is probably payback for what happened

161

the other night onstage," Heath said darkly. "But that guy messed with the wrong band."

"You have to postpone the video," Zander begged. "I can't be recorded looking like this."

"We can't cancel. Everything is ready to go, the extras are lined up, and money is on the line," Briggs said. He touched Kyle's head. "Maybe we can work the hair dye into the video story line."

"How?" Kyle asked.

"I'll talk to the director and think of something," Briggs promised. "Just finish getting styled and get out there."

"But—" Zander protested.

"No buts. Just get ready." Briggs sounded

agitated. "And, Mac? You should probably go so they can work faster."

I didn't even get my makeup or hair done yet! It didn't seem like anyone cared about that at the moment, though. Did this mean I wasn't an extra anymore? Was Kyle mad at me, even though I hadn't done anything wrong? I wasn't sure.

All I could think was that Madam Celeste was a very wise psychic.

And I hated her for it.

LOCATION: Williamsburg, Virginia

SCARLET'S CELL: This one is REALLY bad.

As soon as I saw Scarlet's text, I knew: Bad Kitty was back with another vlog, and it was going to be a smelly batch of kitty litter. Jilly and I hovered over my phone on the hotel room bed and watched her latest video.

"Hey, kitty cats, this is Bad Kitty here with today's gossip! Who were those ridiculous bleach boys filming a video in Love Park in Philadelphia recently? We hear it's none other than Perfect Storm, and their *shoot was so disastrous we doubt they'll be invited back for a cheesesteak anytime soon. The guys were said to be difficult. Apparently they insisted on doing their own hair, which took a wrong turn when the guys picked up bleach instead of shampoo! Meow! If that wasn't bad enough, they left their fans hanging for hours before finally emerging to shoot a scene with extras. The guys didn't even stop for autographs after filming! What bratty boy banders! What do you expect from guys who sleep with Tigger stuffed animals—Heath!—are afraid of green foods and drinks—Zander!—and talk to their mamas five times a day on their phones—Kyle! In other news, Thunder and Lightning continues to take the music world by storm with its latest—"*

I paused the video with shaky fingers and looked at Jilly. "She's lying about the video

166

shoot—the guys had to rework the story line, which is why they filmed so long they had no time for autographs—but she's right about the personal stuff," I admitted. "Jilly, those things are written in my journal!"

"Even the part about Kyle talking to his mom five times a day?" Jilly asked. "That part sounded made up."

"It's not. Kyle just told me that the other day when I saw him texting with a Kiki—that's the name he stores his mom under in his phone. He was sort of embarrassed about it, but I thought it was cute and I"—my voice gave out—"wrote it in my journal."

"Huh." Jilly began to bite a strand of her hair, which was her new habit. "I had no idea Kyle was such a momma's boy. It's kind of cute. But Bad Kitty shouldn't know that. How does she know that? Mikey G. has your journal when you don't have it on you!"

"I know!" I threw my head back on the hotel's

luxurious triple pillows. "I only take my journal back from him to write in it." (Like now.) "Then I give it right back to him." I looked at Jilly. "There's no way someone would know he keeps it in his *Life After Life* DVD case unless they saw him put it in there." I handed her a pack of gum from my pocket, and she stopped sucking on her hair to pop a piece in her mouth.

"Mikey G. is too smart to let someone spy on him," Jilly said, chewing loudly. "I'm sure she didn't get any of this info from your journal. It's just not possible. Try not to freak out."

I didn't know what I'd do if I didn't have Jilly to talk to. Mom had her hands full with this crazy boy band tour. Iris and Scarlet were far away and consumed with PS Social Media Command Central, and Kyle and the guys were killing themselves trying to finish their album on the road and come up with a new single. Sometimes I felt a little like that PS boat lost at sea on the album cover I created for the band a few months back.

Then Jilly would appear like a tugboat and pull me back to shore.

"But you didn't see Kyle's face the other day at the video shoot," I said, thinking back. "He looked like he blamed me for Jeremy getting in the makeup trailer."

"That's crazy!" Jilly said, popping a huge bubble. "Both bands are getting out of control with all this pranking!"

The tricks had intensified since the video

shoot. First, a delivery guy from a local pizza place in Boston knocked on Jeremy and Cody's hotel room door at two AM with twenty pizzas that they hadn't ordered. (That prank had Heath written all over it.) Then, in Baltimore, Zander had a freak-out when he arrived at the Sizzling Summer Boys concert and found every food and drink in the greenroom, was, well, green, the color he deeply fears. "But you requested all green foods on your rider!" the concert venue manager had said as Zander ran from the room like he was being chased by the Roaring Dragon himself. Mom said she was starting to feel like a babysitter at an unruly preschool. No matter how much she threatened or pleaded, the pranks kept escalating, and somehow Bad Kitty knew about all of them—and more.

I heard my phone ping again. Scarlet and Iris were back with their daily social media status report.

IRIS'S CELL: T and L's followers doubled this week while PS's only went up by a few hundred.

SCARLET'S CELL: How are we going to stop Bad Kitty? She has all these posts about how great T and L are, and for some reason she's trying to destroy PS! She wrote Zander's biggest fear in life is going bald. Like that could ever happen!

Jilly and I looked at each other. "I wrote that in my journal last week," I said. "Zander told me that secret when I bought him that pricey shampoo to help restore his natural hair color. The only person I told was you."

"I'm your best friend! I would never tell anyone!" Jilly said defensively.

"I know, but someone did," I said worriedly. "How is Bad Kitty finding these things out?"

"Shh!" Jilly jumped up from the bed and

scanned the room with a look that reminded me of her *Mac Attack* alter ego. "Aha!" She pulled a picture of Colonial Williamsburg off the wall. All that was behind it was more yellow wallpaper. "Huh. Nothing."

"What are you doing?" I whispered.

"Looking for bugs," Jilly said. "Someone is clearly bugging you. It happened on *I Am We* the other night." That is Jilly's favorite sci-fi show. She ran over and began searching my arms and legs like my mom does after I've been in high grass somewhere that could have ticks. "I don't see any electronic thingies, though." Her eyes widened. "Do you think someone could have implanted a device in you while you were sleeping?"

Had this sort of thing ever happened on *Life After Life?* There had been evil twins and mistaken identities, but as far as I could remember, no one had ever been implanted with a tracker. That was ludicrous. I felt my throat for lumps, then checked behind my ears. "They better not have!"

Jilly nodded. "It would probably be too hard to do to you when your mom shares a room." Her face darkened. "But you can never be too careful."

I might never sleep again.

Both of our phones buzzed. There were more texts from PS Social Media Command Central. It's no wonder Briggs actually liked having my friends unofficially on staff. We knew what the world was saying about Perfect Storm before even the label did.

IRIS'S CELL: Bad Kitty is reporting Heath's mom took his credit card away after all those

173

pizzas were delivered to T and L's hotel room. She said he'd been abusing his card and couldn't have it for a few weeks.

SCARLET'S CELL: We know that report is true because you're the one who texted us that, Mac!!!

Gulp. I wrote that in my journal and texted it to the girls, too! I tapped my phone. "Could our phones be bugged?"

"I don't know," Jilly said, feeling the sides of her phone for I didn't know what. "Someone knows what you've been saying and writing." She rubbed her chin. "You know I love Mikey G., but can we really trust him? Somehow info that only you know is leaking from your guarded journal. The only way that could happen is if Bad Kitty compromised Mikey G., overheard us talk, or hacked our phones, or you've been implanted with a recording device."

I held my throat again in horror. "I have not been implanted with a recorder!"

IRIS'S CELL: Do you think our phones have been hacked???

Oh no, not them, too!

"It can't be my journal," I stressed. "Mikey G. is solid." I was sure of that. He loved the guys and would never betray them. "Bad Kitty must be finding these things out another way. I'm not the only one who knows their secrets," I pointed out. "They must confide in other people, too."

"Like who?" Jilly asked. "When you're famous, everyone wants something from you. That's what Daddy says. Perfect Storm has to be careful who they let into their inner circle. You're like family now. They trust you like they trust me."

I had reached the inner circle. Being this close to Perfect Storm was something I only ever dreamed about. And now it was happening.

Circle
of
trust

Heath and Zander were like brothers to me. Kyle and I could (fingers crossed!) have a future in Paris. All that would go up in smoke if I didn't figure out how Bad Kitty was learning their secrets.

I grabbed Jilly's hand. "How long is PS going to continue to trust me when they realize all their secrets are becoming public? They'll start to blame me and then—" I gasped. "They'll kick Mom and me off the tour."

"NO WAY," Jilly said angrily. "I'm not going to let that happen! There's only one solution: We have to find out who Bad Kitty is and put her back in her crate!"

I hung my head. "Good luck. Her disguise is so good you can't tell who she is."

Jilly pulled her long hair up into a bun with a pencil. "I know a lot of people through Daddy. I'll investigate. I'm not going to let some fur ball ruin you."

SCARLET'S CELL: Guys? U still there?

IRIS'S CELL: How are we going to stop Bad Kitty? I really think you have to call in to The Morning Mash Up! Let the guys tell everyone what's really going on!

SCARLET'S CELL: And in the meantime, what do you want us to do at command central?

I needed to channel Mac Attack and figure

177

out if someone was reading my journal. Jilly was going to unmask Bad Kitty before it was too late. We had a lot to do and not a lot of time in which to do it. I texted back the girls.

MY CELL: Hang tight! Jilly and I have a plan.

I didn't have an actual plan yet, but I would get one fast.

I heard the key card slide into the door.

"Someone might be breaking in to torture you for your secrets!" Jilly said in horror. "It happened on *I Am We* the other night."

I got into tae kwon do position and thought of Mac Attack. "That won't happen!"

The door opened slowly, and I held my breath.

Mom poked her head in. "Hi, girls!"

Jilly flopped back down on the bed and took deep breaths.

"What are you up to?" Mom asked curiously.

"Worrying about spies," Jilly mumbled.

"What?" Mom had on workout clothes, and her short brown hair was pulled back, making her look young enough to be my big sister. "You two look miserable. You need to enjoy this gorgeous day! Guess what I have for you? Hurricane Harbor water park passes!" Mom held out bright blue passes with a wave on them.

Jilly's mood immediately lifted. "Cool!"

"Hurricane Harbor heard Perfect Storm talking about how hot it is here in Virginia when they were on Sizzle 106.3 this morning, and they called Briggs to offer everyone tickets to the park," Mom explained. "I think all the guys are going and some of the roadies, too, since everyone has the day off."

I pulled the water park website up on my phone while Mom continued to talk. It said CHILLAX and had a picture of a girl spinning around in a tube with her eyes closed. Maybe I could chillax on the lazy river and forget all about Bad Kitty

179

and how she was finding out PS's innermost secrets. Plus it was a water park, which meant NO SHARKS!

"Let's go, Mac," Jilly said, bouncing up and down on the hotel bed. I heard my phone buzz.

KYLE'S CELL: I hear you might be joining us at Hurricane Harbor.

KYLE'S CELL: Hoping that's true because I need a tubing partner. Heath and Zander always pair up and leave me the odd mate out. ☹

An emoji sad face from Kyle? The thought of Kyle and me sharing a tube all day?

How could I say no?

LOCATION: Still Williamsburg, Virginia*
(*I had to borrow my journal again because so much happened today! Mikey G. agreed to stand outside my room while I wrote, so here it goes...)

An hour and a half later (after hiding my journal again), Mikey G. escorted Perfect Storm, Jilly, and me to Hurricane Harbor for the full VIP Chillax experience! We had our own cabana to retreat to between rides, and it was equipped with lounge chairs, a tub full of soft drinks, and a FREE souvenir table that had towels, water bottles, sunglasses, and sunblock with HURRICANE HARBOR stamped on them. Alec, our Hawaiian shirt–wearing guide, said we could also order food to the cabana so that we didn't have to wait in line with all the park guests!

"So you're saying if I wanted to order a double

cheeseburger with chili cheese fries at ten AM, I could?" Heath asked. He was wearing a tank top and a pair of board shorts covered in variously colored skulls. "Because I'm starved."

"Mate, can we save the stomach-churning eats for after we go on the Drop and Roll?" Kyle asked. "I do not want you throwing up on me on the one-hundred-and-eighty-foot slide."

Zander took a seat on a lounge chair underneath a fake palm tree. Even though our cabana was private, it hadn't stopped girls who'd heard Perfect Storm was coming from crowding around outside and straining to get a picture. Zander took off his sunglasses, removed his shirt (to giant screams), and laid down. "Tell me how the ride is. I don't want to get my hair wet."

Heath groaned. "Dude, your hair is not going to turn orange again."

Zander opened one blue eye and looked at Heath. "It might. My hair is just back to its natural brown after all that processing. Simone, my hair reconstructionist, says I have to be careful it doesn't get brittle. No chlorine."

"What the heck is a hair reconstructionist?" Heath said. "Dude, your hair is fine." He rummaged through the souvenirs and threw Zander a green swim cap that said HH. "Put this on."

Zander stared at it curiously. We all started throwing out encouragement so he'd put it on. The cap was so tight it almost pulled his eyes into his forehead. He stood up and puffed out his chest. "How does it look?"

"Brill, mate," Kyle said, and winked at me, which made my fingers tingle. If he was winking, then he wasn't mad about the latest Bad Kitty vlog. Or he hadn't seen it yet. "Only you could pull that look off." Kyle had on a rash guard like Heath's except his was bright yellow (and his swim trunks had surfboards on them).

"They said you guys have your pick of rides," Mikey G. told us. "They'll clear them out so you can avoid the lines whenever you say the word." He was munching on one of those WHEY OUT! bars again.

"Dude, what is that nasty smell?" Zander asked.

Mikey G. stopped chewing. "My WHEY OUT! bars. You should know. You sent them to me."

Zander made a face. "They smell awful. I would never send you those things."

"Really?" Mikey G. looked like he was thinking this through. "But the card was signed 'Your favorite people.' A big box of them was delivered to the front desk."

"Speaking of big, the Kahuna slide is massive, and I'm dying to get on it." Heath rubbed his hands together excitedly. "Or maybe we can try the Toilet Bowl."

"The toilet bowl?" Jilly and I repeated.

"The ride that spins you around, then drops you into another tube like a giant toilet bowl," said Heath.

"Gross!" Jilly wrapped her new Hurricane Harbor beach towel around her waist. "What else can we go on? How about the wave pool?"

"Wave pool!" I chimed in. Anything but a ride Heath had dubbed "the toilet bowl." I started jumping up and down and waving my hands like I was trying to get Krissy's attention in tutoring. Kyle mimicked me.

"Okay, let's hit the wave pool," Heath said, and the rest of us cheered.

"Let me call over and have it cleared," said Alec, pulling out his walkie-talkie.

"We don't need a pool cleared," Kyle said, and the guys looked at him. "People paid to come here. We can't put them out. Mikey G. can keep things under control."

Zander looked a tad disappointed. "I don't want anyone to see my swim cap."

"We'll send extra security just in case you need it," Alec told us.

Kyle was right. Mikey G. and some Hurricane Harbor lifeguards were a perfect barrier between the guys and any overly excited fans asking to share a tube with them in the wave pool. Once the alarm sounded, people started to scream in excitement and swim off anyway. Within seconds, giant waves began coming out of the tiki huts at the far end of the pool. The waves lifted you up, then dropped you down again, going from really big to really small every few seconds. Heath and Jilly swam all the way out to the huts to fight the biggest waves. Zander was hesitant at first, but he wound up swimming over to some fans who told him they loved his swim cap, and Kyle and I hung out in the section where we could stand when a wave didn't crash over our heads.

"So this is"—Kyle's head was swallowed up by a wave—"cool, huh?"

"Yes! I'm just happy we don't have to see"—I went under myself—"Lightning," I said when I came up for air.

Kyle's smile clouded over. "Now that the pranks have started, I think things are going to get worse instead of better. I'm just glad you"—my head went underwater again and I missed half of Kyle's sentence—"back."

Back? Back what? Had Kyle's back? I didn't feel like I did lately. Kyle was looking at me like I was supposed to say something, which made me start to panic. Did he say "chillax," which sounds like "back"? I opened my mouth wide and shouted, "THIS IS—" And a giant wave took me out. I swallowed half the pool, choking on the chlorine as I went under. I felt Kyle reach out to grab me. He helped me to the shallow end, where I continued to hack up pool water.

"Are you okay?" Kyle patted me on the back like I was choking. How embarrassing! In the distance, I heard a whistle. Little did I know it was Mikey G. with a warning.

"Aww, did the baby swallow too much pool water?"

I wiped water from my eyes and saw Lola Cummings, who was wearing a black bikini that looked like it belonged on the cover of a magazine. I was in a blue-and-white-striped swim tee that said LOVE in the same color pink as my swim bottoms.

"Mackenzie, didn't your mom ever get you swim lessons?" Lola asked. "Maybe you should go back to the hotel so she can take you shopping for pool floaties." The bestie and babysitter giggled behind her.

Kyle helped me up. "Were you looking for someone, Lola?" He was trying to sound polite, but I could hear the edge to his voice. It made me giddy to think he didn't like Big Bird, either.

"You guys, of course," Lola said brightly. "We haven't hung out in for-EVER."

She touched Kyle's arm, and I prayed for a rogue wave to knock her down.

"That's why I flew in for tomorrow night's show," Lola continued. "I miss you guys! I checked into the same hotel and ran into Briggsy in the lobby…"

Why did Lola get to call Briggs Briggsy? He hated when I called him that.

"He gave us passes for the water park to meet up with you guys." She held out her cell phone, which was in one of those waterproof cases. "Selfie!" Lola grabbed one of her and an annoyed-looking Kyle before I could stop her.

191

@lolacummings 37m

300 people like this
Chillin with @kylebeyer #Summer #blessed

I heard the alarm go off again, and the waves died down. People started to make their way out of the pool, including Zander and a bunch of female fans.

"Where to next?" he said as girls snapped pictures. If anyone could pull off that ridiculous swim cap, it was Zander. "Oh, hey, Lola. What are you doing here?"

Lola blinked rapidly. "Don't I get a hug?" She pouted.

Zander motioned to himself. "I'm kind of all wet," he said as girls all around him started begging for hugs, too.

Heath and Jilly came running out of the water. Jilly scowled when she saw our archenemy. Well, my archenemy, but as one of my best friends, she

192

took the role on herself, too. "I heard Hurricane Harbor has something called Shark Bait," Heath said. "Want to go?"

"That attraction has limited tickets, but guess what? I already put all your names down for the eleven AM spots because I knew you'd want to do it," Lola said, then looked at me and Jilly. "Even yours."

"Sweet!" said Heath.

She held her arms open for a hug, and Heath blew past her.

Shark Bait. I didn't like the sound of a ride that had the word "shark" in the title.

"What is Shark Bait, anyway?" I heard Bridget ask Lola in between pops of gum. "Do we have partners? I call Zander."

Lola stopped short. "Hello? If we have partners, I get Zander." Bridget frowned. "And Shark Bait isn't a ride. It's their new shark tank experience. We get to swim with sharks! Is that AH-MAZING or what?"

"Swim with sharks?" I repeated meekly.

"Small ones," Kyle assured me. "They couldn't eat you." He grinned. "Well, unless you looked like a super-tasty snack."

Kyle was kidding. Right? RIGHT?

"Awesomesauce!" Heath said, stopping for a second to sign an autograph on a girl's beach towel before Mikey G. waved her away. She ran off screaming happily.

My ears had a whooshing sound in them, and I was suddenly very cold. *The Sharkinator Returns* flashed in my head. I could have sworn there was a scene in a water park. Wasn't there? When sharks got loose and flooded a lazy river and ate people? "Sharks eat people!" I shouted as they kept walking.

"Please," Lola snorted. "Don't be such a baby, Mackenzie."

"Why would we want to swim with sharks when we already have one here?" Jilly asked.

"Hang back if you want. I'm sure the guys

194

won't notice." Lola slid her giant sunglasses off her face and onto her head.

"I'm not sure the guys would miss you, either, Lola," Jilly said, pointing to the boys, who were racing in front of us. Lola's eyebrows furrowed. "I think we've spoken to you more than they have."

Lola looked at Bridget and began to stutter. "I… well…" She growled. "Sometimes I can't stand them!" she yelled, and I couldn't believe what I was hearing. "I mean, I can't stand you two," she snapped. "If you're scared, you can go sit on a lounge chair and write about your fears in your little journal." Bridget's gum popped in agreement.

Jilly's head whipped around. "What did you just say?"

I was so mad, I spoke over Jilly. I tried to think like Mac Attack. "I'm not scared. I'm going because the guys actually want me there." I pushed ahead of her to walk with Kyle. Being Kyle's partner was the whole reason I had wanted to go to Hurricane Harbor. I couldn't let him down.

Lola was laughing like a hyena as she ran ahead of me and hooked arms with Zander. When would that boy learn? "There it is! Shark Bait!"

I saw the great white shark hanging as a sign in front of a tiki hut and stopped. SHARK BAIT was written on the shark in what looked like—GULP—blood.

"Are you sure you're okay?" Kyle asked as my right eye began to twitch.

"Fine. Not getting eaten," I mumbled as I took

the steps to the attraction two at a time, walking through the hut and toward a pool that had a half-sunk pirate ship in it. I stared at the coral on the sandy bottom and saw things moving. BIG things moving. I jumped backward, banging into a guy in a wet suit. "Sorry." Wait. I recognized that cranky look.

"What are you doing here?" Jeremy zipped up his wet suit. "This session is booked."

"Hey, Jeremy!" Lola cooed, her arm firmly linked with Zander's. "Isn't this great? I registered Heath, Kyle, Zander, and their little friends to do Shark Bait, too."

"You said this was our thing." Jeremy eyed Heath, who gave him the stink eye back. "Why would you invite these guys? You said they've been ignoring you."

"Jeremy!" Lola laughed, hanging on Zander, who was trying to pull away. "What are you talking about? Let's put all that bad blood aside and have fun today. Besides, Hurricane Harbor wants to take promotional photos of both your bands for their website."

How did Lola know that? Was she a publicist now, too?

Jeremy growled. "I don't trust them. This morning they hid alarm clocks all over my hotel room that went off every five minutes from four AM to six."

Heath stifled a laugh. "I have no idea how that happened." He grimaced. "Or how *someone* poured mac and cheese powder into our orange juice containers on the bus."

"Beats having room service send up caramel-covered ONIONS," Jeremy said.

"Or someone replacing all the gummy bears in the greenroom with sugar-free ones." Zander blushed. "They make you...Well, let's just say I cleared out a room."

Jeremy grinned. "Works every time. It also makes you ripe for retaliation. There is no way

I'm getting in a shark tank with you guys. One of you will try to get me eaten."

"See?" I panicked to Jilly. "Even small sharks *do* eat people!"

"It's up to you, Jer," Lola said, "but I'm going with Zander. The Hurricane Harbor photographer is already waiting in the water to take our picture, but if you don't need the social media love, stay on dry land."

I couldn't believe it when Jeremy listened to her. He mumbled something I couldn't hear, grabbed a snorkel mask and fins, then waited at the pool steps.

No one else backed down, either. Jilly ignored my shark warnings and started looking through wet suits for one that fit. The park employees helped the guys get ready. One of the workers approached me, but I waved him off. "What if we're the first people to try this tank?" I asked Jilly. "If they haven't figured out the sharks'

feeding schedule yet, they might get hungry and take a nibble of my big toe."

Jilly held up her footwear. "You're wearing flippers."

"Sharks can eat through shoes!" I reminded her. "In *The Sharkinator Returns*, one shark ate a whole gas pump! Then he blew up, but still."

Kyle walked over to us. "Do you need help finding a wet suit? I can't believe you're going. Way to fight the fear, Mac."

Kyle was smiling at me in a way that made

my heartbeat slow down. I focused on Kyle's gleaming teeth and saw a picture of the two of us walking along the Champs-Élysées in Paris talking about the day everything changed between us. "I knew you were the girl for me when I saw you jump in the shark tank that day in Virginia," Kyle would say. "It made me realize how brave you were." Then I'd say, "I channeled my comic book alter ego Mac Attack and knew a little leopard shark wasn't going to keep me from swimming with you." Then Kyle would take my hand and say—

"Do you need flippers?" Kyle waved a pair of smelly black ones in my face.

"Oh!" I held my nose. "Maybe I should try them on over there on that bench."

I could hear the Shark Bait guy explaining the rules to everyone already in their wet suits. I was the only one not wearing one yet. Something about swimming slowly across, no horseplay, how the water was a cool sixty-eight degrees. Why wasn't he talking about shark safety?

"You're not going, either?" Cody walked over. He looked sweaty and nervous, and it made me wonder if he had shark fears, too.

"I'm undecided," I said warily, as I didn't want Heath to see me talking to him.

Cody sat down next to me. He didn't even

have a bathing suit on. "They've got an octopus in the tank. I'm allergic to calamari, so I didn't think it was a good idea if I swam with anything else with tentacles."

Why didn't I try an excuse like that? *I'm allergic to sharks.* That would solve all my saltwater-based dilemmas. I had to remember this conversation.

I became momentarily distracted when I saw Jeremy walk over to Lola and Zander. "I want to go with Lola," he said.

"I'm going with Za—" Lola started to say at the same time Zander said: "She's all yours. No offense, Lola. I'd rather head out with an instructor."

"But, but…" Lola looked after him mournfully.

"Told you so," Jeremy smirked. Lola hit him in the arm of his wet suit.

Did Jeremy have a thing for Lola? I almost felt sorry for the boy if he did.

"Heath and Jilly are teamed up, so that leaves me and Mac," Kyle said as he turned to me, eyeing Cody again. "What do you think? Will you be okay out there? I really don't want to make you wait here alone."

Kyle meant he didn't want me saying anything that could compromise Perfect Storm. Well, he didn't have to worry. My fear of sharks had rendered me speechless. "I...I..." I started shaking my head vehemently. Cody was looking at me now, too. "I'm...not...sure..."

"I'll go with you, Kyle," Bridget said. In their matching wet suits and flippers, they looked like a couple from a comic book. Bridget had Princess Leia braids high on her head that only made her look more sci-fi. I was not happy. I tried to shoot her a few lasers with my eyes, which were the only part of my body still working.

"Well, if Mac's not going...," he started to say, but I could tell he was disappointed. So was I. What if Bridget was the one who wound up walking along the Champs-Élysées with Kyle instead of me and it all came down to this moment? My heart was revving when I saw Heath and Jilly slide into the pool. Zander was next, then Lola and Jeremy. I heard Lola give a scream when she hit the water.

"Sorry," I managed to blurt out. I was sorry. *For so many things*, I wanted to add.

"Me too," Kyle said with a shrug, and then he walked into the shark-infested waters without me.

LOCATION: The sun*
*At least that's how hot it feels in Savannah, Georgia, right now!

When Briggs came onto the bus coughing and gasping, we all panicked.

"Dad!" Jilly jumped up from the heated game of Heads Up! we were playing with the guys.

Mom came running, like moms usually do at the sound of screaming, and had her arms around Briggs's waist before we all could even figure out what was going on. She was attempting to do the Heimlich when Briggs quit coughing and started yelling at us.

"I'm fine! BLECH! Fine! BLECH!" Briggs said between gagging fits. He ran to the fridge and popped open the first drink he found, which

was an orange Roaring Dragon. His face relaxed as he drank it. Then he turned and looked at us. His face was filled with fury. "Who. Put. Horse-radish. In. The. Vanilla. Cream. Doughnuts?"

"Oops," Heath muttered. "Briggsy, those dough-nuts weren't meant for you. Thunder and Light-ning was supposed to eat them. Vanilla cream is Jeremy's favorite."

"How do you know that?" Zander asked.

Heath shrugged. "I've been doing my research. Jeremy must be doing his, too, or he wouldn't have thought to put toothpaste in my Oreos."

"This has got to stop!" Mom reprimanded the boys. "Look what's happening. You're not just hurting each other; now you're... burning your manager's mouth."

Jilly started to giggle, which set off the rest of us. Neither Mom nor Briggs was amused. They sounded like total parents. Just then we heard banging on the door. Mom opened it, and Mikey G. walked in with a huge box of WHEY OUT! bars. "I heard yelling. All okay? What did I miss?"

"We tried to prank Thunder and Lightning, but got Briggsy instead," Heath said.

Mikey G. held his heart while trying to balance the box of WHEY OUT! bars on one hand. "But you're all okay? Thank God. I had to go to the front desk of the hotel to get this package.

Glad you guys were here, actually. It's impossible to open the door to the bus when you're holding a box this heavy."

"We're fine," Briggs said, "but we won't be if one of these pranks injures someone. The press will have a field day!"

"They already do. Bad Kitty blames everything bad on us," Zander said. "Or she tells her viewers something embarrassing about us, like how I use a facial steamer at night to soothe my vocal cords."

Heath cracked up. "That is embarrassing."

Zander glared at him. "Maybe you're the one who told her, then." Heath's eyebrows shot up. "The people in this room are the only ones who know that I use one. So which one of you is the traitor?"

"Chill, bro," Heath said. "We've been down this road once already. We're your bandmates. No one is a traitor."

"Someone has to be," Kyle said. "Things on

this tour are right dodgy. You guys are the only ones who know how hard I am trying to come up with a decent song. I can't find the inspiration with everything going on. How does Bad Kitty know that?"

"Guys, remember, The Raven offered you three songs as a replacement for 'The Story of a Girl,'" Briggs said.

"None of those are right, and you know it." Zander dropped onto the couch with a thud. "Nothing's as good as Kyle's original."

"Thanks, mate," Kyle said. "Too bad we lost it somehow. I just wish the world didn't know we were desperate to find a new tune." For a moment, Kyle's eyes flickered to me, and I knew why. He had come to me last week complaining about how slow his songwriting was going. Did he think I blabbed?

"Maybe we should pack up and call off the rest of this tour," Heath said. "Thunder and Lightning is seriously getting inside our heads. We can't write, we're always looking over our shoulders, the press is writing garbage about us. Yesterday Bad Kitty wrote about my stuffed-animal collection! How'd she know I have one?"

"Didn't Zander out you in Vegas last spring?" Jilly asked.

"That was only about my Tigger." Heath's face flamed. "No one knew I have a few other animals I sleep with, too." He coughed and looked away.

"Let's stop with the killing the tour talk." Briggs took another swig of his Roaring Dragon, probably to wash the horseradish taste out of his mouth. "I'm already stressed enough thinking about your Perfect Storm/Thunder and Lightning photo shoot for *Popstar!* today."

Popstar! was here? That was Scarlet's, Iris's, and my favorite magazine! They always had the latest gossip on celebs and included all these foldout posters of stars to hang on our walls.

How cool would it be to have a poster of PS on my wall that was taken at a photo shoot I actually went to?

"They flew into Savannah just to do a spread on the Sizzling Summer Boys Tour, and the label wants you to play nice," Briggs told the guys, who moaned. "You go, smile, say nothing bad about Thunder and Lightning, and you'll be out of there before you know it." Briggs looked at Heath. "If you don't prank each other and screw this up."

Mom walked over to me and Jilly. "I'm counting on you two to help us make things go smoothly. Don't get sweet-talked into discussing anything personal with the *Popstar!* reporters. They may want to interview you about the tour, too."

I squealed. "I'm going to be in a magazine?" I could see my face on the cover of *Popstar!* now. MEET THE GIRL WHO STOLE KYLE BEYER'S HEART! "We're just friends," I would say while Kyle said, "Mac is the—"

"Mac?" Mom was giving me a look that had *Mackenzie Sabrina Lowell* all in the eyes. "If asked, all you say is that the tour is going great and that reports of the bands' not getting along are greatly exaggerated."

"Exaggerated, got it," I repeated.

But the minute we got to the shoot, I knew *Popstar!* reporters would know the truth: Reports of the boy band battle were *not* exaggerated. The guys couldn't stand each other, and the proof was right in front of their eyes.

"I think we should get started," said one of the fashion editors. "We brought some plaid shirts, jeans, killer boots, and Stetsons, of course. When in the South..." He chuckled at his own joke. The guys didn't laugh.

"They'd love to pick out clothes, right, guys?" Briggs said pointedly.

"Yes, Thunder and Lightning, too," said Ronald hurriedly. He waved Jeremy and Cody over to a rack far from Heath, Kyle, and Zander's.

"This could take a while," Jilly told me with a yawn. "Let's explore the place."

The Smokehouse was a famous barbecue joint closed for the shoot, but someone must have leaked this info because girls were pressed up against the windows looking in. A *Popstar!* editor quickly closed the curtains. Jilly and I walked around the restaurant. It was nothing like the picnic table and checkered tablecloth place we had eaten at a few days ago on the road from North Carolina. Here everything was deep mahogany, real wood walls, elk-antler chandeliers, cow print–covered seat benches, and in the middle of the restaurant was a...

"Mechanical bull!" Jilly ran to a fence around the bull to get a closer look. The mechanical bull looked like the real animal, if you forgot the fact it had no legs and there was a handle on his back to hold on to. The bull was surrounded by a mat in case you were thrown off. "I've always wanted to try one."

"Then today is your lucky day." Cody came up behind us in a cranberry plaid shirt, a cowboy hat, and jeans.

We both froze. I wasn't sure we could be seen talking to the enemy, but Cody had been nice to me the other day at Hurricane Harbor. Still, I was on guard. What if he was just being nice to find out information about PS? Maybe he was the mole! (Jilly had really gotten me into this spy theory.)

"The restaurant manager told me the bull has slow settings, so anyone who wants to ride can try it when the shoot is over," Cody told us. "I'd hop on, but last time I tried one, I got thrown off, and it was sort of embarrassing."

"Why are you being nice to us?" Jilly asked pointedly, and I cringed. "You put toothpaste in Heath's Oreos the other day, and I almost threw up when I ate one."

Cody rubbed his forehead, almost knocking off his cowboy hat. "I didn't know you guys were going to taste them, too." He sighed. "I'm sorry. I told Jeremy he was going too far. Now that I know you ate one, I feel really terrible." For a moment, I saw Jilly's attitude flicker.

"Okay, so maybe you're not so bad, but your brother is a major pain!" Jilly said. "And you guys stole PS's favorite song!"

Cody frowned. "We told you—we didn't steal it. When it was given to Jeremy at the recording studio that night we met you, we didn't know the songwriter was Kyle. Jeremy said the song was written for us."

Jilly moved closer. "*Who* told Jeremy that? Did he say who handed him the lyrics?"

Cody blinked. "Well, no, but—"

"Then how do you know your brother is actually telling you the truth?" Jilly sounded like a prosecutor on one of my grandma's law shows! "Couldn't it be possible he stole the song from the PS studio when they were on break? *Think*. Why would they give their favorite song away?"

"I...," Cody started to say, but Jilly cut him off.

"Why would PS be so upset about losing the song if it wasn't stolen?" Jilly pushed.

"I don't know," Cody said. "The guys blew us off that night. They were so rude, and Jeremy said—"

"They weren't rude; they were tired," I explained. "Haven't you ever been tired?" Cody looked at me. "Kyle really cares about his song-writing, and that song was very important to him. Now he'll never get to record it, let alone sing it. Instead, he has to listen to you guys play it over and over on every tour stop. How do you think that makes him feel?"

Cody looked over at Kyle, who was trying on a cowboy hat. "Lousy. I write songs, too, you know. I had no idea—"

"Mac?" Kyle walked toward me wearing a

yellow-and-navy shirt and worn dark jeans. I loved his cowboy hat. He side-eyed Cody. "Everything okay?"

"Fine," Jilly said, and I nodded. "We just had some business to discuss."

"Kyle?" Cody sounded unsure. "Do you think we could talk for a sec?"

"Sorry, mate." The way Kyle said "mate" made me think he was no mate at all. "Kind of busy. Let's go, guys." He steered us both away from Cody, who looked pretty uncomfortable. Well, good! He needed to know all the problems he caused. "How many times do I have to tell you not to talk to him, Mac?" Kyle whispered. "You can't trust those guys."

"Kyle, I—" I'd never heard him so annoyed. "We were trying to help you."

"Let us handle this," Kyle said as an editor started to wave the guys over. He tilted the front of his hat and walked away.

"Geez, talk about overreacting," Jilly said. The groups were in opposite corners, whispering and

223

looking over at each other like they were gossiping in my middle school cafeteria. "He'll get over it."

I wasn't so sure. We watched the photographer set up the first shot from a distance. All five guys posed and smiled like they were best friends as they hung over the restaurant's second-story railing. Then they broke to set up a new shot, and the guys hurried back to opposite corners. It was uncomfortable, and it went on this way for hours.

Then a *Popstar!* editor walked over to the two of us as we sat at a table eating cheese fries. (What can I say? We were hungry, and the restaurant offered food, so...) "You're Mackenzie and Jillian, right?"

"MWH-HUM," I replied, my mouth full of hot cheese.

"I'm Mara," she said, sitting down across from us.

"Fry?" Jilly offered, dipping one in ketchup and holding it out to her.

"No, thanks," she said. "I can't do fried food."

I swallowed my fry. "You're missing out."

Mara smiled. "I had a few questions about being on the road with the two hottest bands of the summer."

"Well, *one* hottest band," Jilly said, and I elbowed her.

"She just means that our loyalty is to Perfect Storm since we're part of their road crew," I said, but Mara was already jotting something down in her notebook. She pulled out a piece of paper and read from it.

"So would you say you're pretty close with the band, Mac, since your mom took over as the boys' tour manager this spring?" Mara pushed her phone across the table, recording our conversation.

"Yes," I said, imagining I was hooked to a polygraph machine.

"You've gotten pretty close to Kyle Beyer, right?" Mara asked. Jilly stared at me, and I could almost hear the warning bells. Stick to the script, Mac!

"I'm close to the whole band," I said nervously. "Both bands, really. So is Jilly. Anything you've heard about their not getting along is untrue. The guys are friends."

"DUDE! That's the shirt I'm wearing in this shot!" we heard Jeremy complain. We looked over and saw that Zander had on the same dark denim button-down Jeremy was wearing.

"I had it on first!" Zander said. "Briggs, tell Jeremy I had it on first!" They sounded like two kids on the playground fighting over a shovel. "You have to change your shirt."

"No, you change shirts!" Jeremy shot back.

Mara laughed. "Sounds like they get along great." Gulp. "So are you and Kyle dating? Or is something going on with you and Cody Callum?"

"WHAT?" I screeched at the same time as Jilly.

"Mac does not like Cody," Jilly said defensively.

Mara slid a picture across the table of Cody

JULY 3 - HURRICANE HARBOR WATER PARK

and me talking at the Shark Bait attraction at Hurricane Harbor. Double gulp.

"That was nothing!" I swore, looking at Jilly, who was frowning. "We were just talking while we waited for the others."

"Navy goes better with my eyes!" I heard Zander yell at Jeremy. Briggs and Mom were waving Zander off. Ronald tried in vain to pull Jeremy away.

"Well, this shirt works with my hair, which

Popstar! online readers just called the coolest boy band cut of the summer," Jeremy told him.

"There is no way their readers would pick your hair over mine!" Zander freaked.

"Our website is even bigger than the magazine," Mara said coolly. "We're the number one teen gossip site on the web." She pointed to the picture of Cody. "We're thinking of putting this picture of you and Cody on there. Unless you have better info on you and Kyle that you want me to use instead."

My jaw dropped. *Popstar!* was my favorite magazine, but they were acting just like Bad Kitty! I couldn't believe it. "Please don't run that picture," I begged. Jilly was squeezing my kneecap so hard I thought it would be black and blue. "It doesn't tell the real story."

Mara shrugged. "You need to give me something if you don't want me to use it."

I searched frantically for Mom to get some

help, but she was busy with Zander and Jeremy, who were now in each other's faces. "I don't have anything."

"I think you do," Mara said. The wheels on her tape recorder were still turning. "Bad Kitty seems to think you know a lot about Perfect Storm."

Bad Kitty was after me now, too?

"You know Bad Kitty?" Jilly asked suspiciously. "Who is she? Where is she from? How do we reach her? Maybe we could work out a deal if you tell us who Bad Kitty really is."

"I don't know how to reach her," Mara said. "But I do get e-mails from her." She showed us a different piece of paper. HOW MACKENZIE LOWELL IS DESTROYING PERFECT STORM BY TELLING ALL THEIR DIRTY LITTLE SECRETS. Bad Kitty was claiming I was the one secretly leaking all these things about Perfect Storm when it was really her!

"This isn't true!" I freaked out. "Bad Kitty is

the one talking trash about PS. Not me! You can't print this!"

"As if you could pull off a cowboy hat," I heard Zander hiss.

"You need one to cover your massive head!" Jeremy spat. "Get the shirt off!"

"Make me!" Zander said.

"We'll bull ride for it," Jeremy told him. "Someone turn on the mechanical bull. The one who stays on the longest gets to wear the shirt."

"Jeremy finally has a good idea!" Heath cheered as Jeremy headed toward the bull-riding area.

"Don't turn on that bull," I heard Briggs beg, but the photographer was already running with a camera.

"I go first!" Zander said, running past Jeremy and jumping the fence to the bull. He hopped on before anyone could stop him.

"Zander, those things are dangerous," Mom said, sounding very Mom. "You could get hurt. And you didn't sign a release to ride it."

Zander ignored her. "I'm ready!" He was holding on so tight his knuckles were red. "Start the bull!"

The Smokehouse was so excited a celebrity was on their bull they didn't argue.

"GO, Z!" Heath shouted as the bull began to rock back and forth. A countdown clock ticked, and everyone in the room started counting. I was still begging.

"You're writing lies," I said, my lip quivering.

"I would never betray PS. Someone is lying to you. I'm not sure how they know the things they do, but I haven't told them to Bad Kitty."

"Sorry," Mara said with a shrug. "If we get a scoop, we have to run with it."

"I think you do know how to reach Bad Kitty," Jilly said, still staring at the page, which Mara tried to pull away. "Give me her e-mail address and I'll give you great gossip." Mara's eyes widened.

Then Zander got thrown from the bull.

"Fifteen seconds!" Heath said.

"Must have been on slow mode," Jeremy said. "Pathetic. Speed mine up."

"I don't think that's a good idea," Ronald said.

"I can handle it," Jeremy insisted, taking a seat on the furry bull and holding on to the seat with one hand.

"What do you know?" Mara asked eagerly, moving the tape recorder Jilly's way.

Loud gasps from around the room kept Jilly from answering. The bull was bucking at a crazy speed. Jeremy, for what it's worth, gave it a good fight—for the six seconds he lasted before he was thrown from the bull into the fence at such speed I was sure he was knocked out. When he sat up, his nose was covered in blood.

Zander laughed. "Whose face is going on the *Popstar!* Hottest Boy of Summer poster now?"

"I think he broke his nose!" Ronald yelled, and Zander stopped laughing. "We need to get him to a doctor." People began running around getting bandages and ice packs.

"This is a disaster!" Mom held her head as the *Popstar!* editors all took pictures of the mayhem and wrote notes.

Briggs held out his phone. "We've got bigger problems. Look at this."

Bad Kitty didn't wait around. She tweeted the scoop she gave Mara herself.

Bad Kitty (•ω•) @bad kitty118 3 min ago
#NEW VIDEO! @PERFECTSTORM BRACING FOR A #HURRICANE. TOUR
MNGRS DAUGHTER SPILLS #PSSECRETS & GETS AWAY WITH IT!

↩   ♺ 3   ☆ 4

Bad Kitty (•ω•) @bad kitty118. now
VLOG POST WITHIN THE HOUR!

↩   ♺   ☆ 2

Friday, July 8—aka
THE NEVER-ENDING DAY

LOCATION: MY WORST NIGHTMARE
(otherwise known as the Hilton, whose ballroom
Mom turned into our Perfect Storm center)

"You told Bad Kitty about my stuffed-animal collection?" Heath freaked out on me.

"And that my fear of the color green started because I was scared of Oscar the Grouch as a kid?" Zander asked.

"My mum is happy that the world knows I call her five times a day," Kyle said to no one in particular. "Me, not so much."

Heath went on. "And that I'm happy to be the background singer because that lets me get away with whatever I want?"

Heath tossed out more things Bad Kitty said I supposedly told her. My eyes welled with tears.

Mom and Briggs were trying to handle the media requests for comments about the fight at the *Popstar!* photo shoot. Jeremy had broken his nose and wouldn't be able to perform for the next few days. I could have sworn I heard Briggs whisper the word "lawsuit," but my mom was way too busy to talk to me. And I was in too much hot water of my own to even ask her.

"How do we know you didn't come on this tour to spy on us?" Zander asked.

"You've got to be kidding," Jilly jumped in. "Are you saying Mac's mom took the job with you guys so her daughter could give information to a sketchy vlogger? Have you guys lost your minds? This is Mac we're talking about!"

Zander looked at me. *Really* looked at me, and frowned again. "How well do we even know Mac? I thought you were our Yoko Ono, but maybe it's more like you're our Yoko No-No."

It was like being punched in the stomach.

"That was harsh," I said. "If you'd just listen…
I didn't give Bad Kitty dirt on you guys! I don't
even know Bad Kitty. Someone is setting me up!"
My life really was becoming like a law show. I
might need to call Grandma for advice when
this conversation ended.

"What about that journal you're always writing in?" Heath asked, and my stomach began to
twist in knots. "Do you write about us?"

They all stared at me. "Yes, but…"

"AHA! So you've written down how I sleep with stuffed tigers and elephants," Heath said.

"Elephants?" Kyle repeated.

Heath blushed. "Dumbo is cool."

"I write about things that happen to me, and sometimes those things include you guys, but my journal is always on me or being guarded," I explained.

"Guarded?" Kyle asked.

"You guys don't have to worry. Mikey G. hangs on to it for her," Jilly said. "Mac has been super careful since her journal went missing that night at the recording studio when Thunder and Lightning stole your song." She covered her mouth in horror.

Everyone got quiet except me. "JILLY!"

"Sorry!" Jilly backpedaled. "It was only lost for a few minutes, I think."

But it was too late. All the guys were yelling, and I was yelling back. We were talking over each other, and I couldn't even make out what anyone was saying till I heard Kyle speak up.

"Did you have the lyrics for 'The Story of a Girl' in your journal?" Kyle asked quietly. Everyone stopped talking and looked at me. That's when I cracked.

"Yes," I said in a wobbly voice. Kyle's face fell, and Zander and Heath exhaled sharply. "But it was only gone a few minutes. My mom grabbed it when she went back to get something. I don't think they got the lyrics from my journal."

"But you don't know for sure," Heath pointed out.

"Guys, you're acting crazy," Jilly said. "Mac was the one who helped you get back together a few months ago! Now you think she's trying to sabotage you? Bad Kitty is the one trying to destroy you—not Mac—and I'm *thisclose* to figuring out who that cat is. I just need a few more hours to do it."

Jilly was on to Bad Kitty? She hadn't said a word to me about this. Then again, we had been kind of busy with the worst *Popstar!* photo shoot ever and the mechanical-bull disaster.

"When we find out who she is, I'm sure all this stuff will make sense." Jilly looked fierce. "We are taking Bad Kitty down. She's the real enemy!"

Zander ignored her. "It had to be your journal. You were the only other person who had the lyrics that night. We took the other copies with us when we left the studio. We aren't stupid enough to leave them hanging around."

"Stupid?" My eyes twitched. The band I loved more than almost anything else in this world (other than Mom, Iris, Scarlet, and Jilly, of course) was looking at me with such anger, I couldn't stand to be in the same room as them. Especially not when I saw Kyle's face. It said it all. Madam Celeste had seen the storm coming, and I had completely ignored it. "You guys don't trust me."

"Mac...," Jilly started to say.

"No, it's true," I said shakily. "It doesn't matter what I tell you right now. You guys don't trust me." Heath looked at his fingernails, which were painted a deep purple. "I thought after all the time we'd spent on the road together, you knew I always had your backs." Zander stared at the ceiling. "But I guess I'm just another fan."

"Mac," Kyle tried to butt in.

"Maybe that's what I should go back to being."

243

My lips quivered. "Maybe it would be a good idea if I left the tour."

I waited to see if one of them would protest. To see if Kyle would throw himself across the table and shout "NOOOOOO!" Instead, all I could hear was Briggs and Mom on their phones. They had no idea what the guys and I were talking about.

"We'll cover Jeremy's hospital bills," we heard Briggs say. "Do whatever it takes to keep that nose of his from winding up in a Bad Kitty vlog. That kitty is going to ruin all our careers!"

I knew the boys thought this was my fault. "I'm out of here." I rushed out of the room before they could see me cry and went up an escalator to the main lobby of the hotel. It was crowded with people. A high school band was in town for a competition. A convention had just let out, and people in suits with shiny name tags walked by talking about where they could eat. I just wanted to disappear. Where could I go? My hotel room was the first place they'd look.

"Hey, Mac! You okay?" I ran into Mikey G. carrying a huge box of WHEY OUT! bars.

"I'm fine." I wiped away my tears. "Don't say you saw me, okay?" Mikey G. nodded. "I just need some peace and quiet to think."

"You can have the bus to yourself if you want," Mikey G. said. "I'm on my way there to drop off these bars and then the place is all yours." He shifted the large box in his arms. "I could use the help getting on the bus actually." He blushed. "These WHEY OUT! boxes are so huge, I can't open the door by myself. I have to leave the bus unlocked when I go pick up a delivery so I can just nudge the door open when I get back and get inside."

"You leave the bus unlocked?" I said slowly.

"For ten minutes max," Mikey G. reassured me. "And only when I get a WHEY OUT! bar delivery. I have no clue who is sending me these things, but I love that they come every week like clockwork! I have four cases on the bus already!"

THAT WAS IT! The tour bus was unlocked.

That had to be how Bad Kitty was getting her hands on my journal, and the bus was unlocked right now! I could catch that kitty in the act if I hurried! "I'll meet you at the bus!" I yelled to Mikey G., and then I pushed my way through the crowd again, banging into a boy carrying a tuba, and hit the button for the elevators to go down to the garage. The tour buses were all parked on the lower level.

I could have sworn I heard someone calling my name, but I had to be wrong.

I was in PS exile. Heath was probably having Briggs make up WANTED posters with my mug on it. When the elevator opened, I jumped inside and hit the close button frantically, but the elevator wouldn't listen. It took its sweet time, and that's when someone's pale arm appeared between the closing doors.

"Mac!" Kyle was out of breath. "I've been chasing you"—DEEP BREATHING—"through the lobby. Blimey, you're fast." The doors shut behind him.

"Just go back to the guys and leave me alone," I said, but it was too late. The elevator whisked us away from the loud lobby, and I grew silent. I could hear the sound of Kyle's shallow breathing. I don't think the boy ran much. "I would never give Thunder and Lightning your song," I blurted out. "You wrote it for me! Why would I want stupid Jeremy and Cody Callum singing it instead of you?!"

Kyle touched my arm. "I know you didn't give them my song. I don't think you talked to Bad Kitty about us, either."

"I didn't— What did you just say?" I stopped yelling. "You believe me?"

"Of course I believe you," Kyle said. "That's what I told the guys before I ran after you. I said, 'Mac is the most loyal mate we've got, and we

248

should trust her over some vlogger we don't even know.'" Kyle's eyes were magnetic, and I couldn't stop staring. "I know you'd never want someone else singing your song. Even if T and L did find lyrics in your journal, it was an accident. You guard that thing with your life." He looked at our shoes. "I just hate that the song was written for you and now that jerk Cody gets to sing it instead."

Aww...was Kyle jealous of Cody? Did that mean Kyle could possibly, maybe, just a smidge, like me as more than a friend?

I grabbed Kyle's hand before I could overthink it. "Then let him sing it. You're going to write an even better song, and when you do, I want to be the first one who hears it." We stood there and grinned goofily at each other until the elevator doors opened. I could hear someone singing in the distance. I almost forgot why I was rushing down here in the first place. To catch Bad Kitty!

249

Kyle frowned. "Do you hear someone singing my song?"

I pulled Kyle out of the elevator to listen. No doubt about it. It was Jeremy Callum! Was he Bad Kitty? "If he's in so much pain from breaking his nose, should he really be singing?" I wondered aloud.

Kyle grabbed my arm, and we quietly made our way behind parked cars until we got close enough to the tour buses to see. Kyle pulled us behind a minivan, where we had a perfect view. There was Jeremy Callum in a red hoodie. He was black and blue around his nose, but he was clearly well enough to stand outside the Perfect Storm tour bus and sing "The Story of a Girl"!

I watched as Jeremy knocked on the door to the PS tour bus. "Hurry up!" I heard him hiss. "He'll be back soon."

Mikey G. was probably still struggling with

his WHEY OUT! bars, and I realized Jeremy knew that, too. He must have been the one sending Mikey G. the bars in the first place. It was all starting to make sense!

"Calm down! I've got it." A girl in a black hoodie walked off the tour bus carrying the *Life After Life* DVD case. It was Bad Kitty, and it was clear that she knew Jeremy and they both knew exactly where to go to find dirt on Perfect Storm!

"MY JOURNAL!" I whisper-shouted. I took a leap forward, and Kyle held me back. He covered my mouth with his free hand, and we watched as Jeremy and Bad Kitty started flipping through my journal pages, taking pictures of the new entries with her camera phone. When they were done, they stuck the journal back in the DVD case, and Bad Kitty put it back inside the tour bus.

I was so angry I could have breathed fire. Jeremy and Bad Kitty were working together! The picture was becoming clear now. Jeremy hated Perfect Storm as much as Bad Kitty did. Now they were using my journal entries (which are written out of love, I might add) to try to destroy my favorite band!

It was time to confront them. "I need to see who is under that hood," I whispered, trying to get away from Kyle (for probably the first and only time in my life!).

"Think for a second!" Kyle whispered in my ear (IN MY EAR!). "We need proof. And backup.

We can't take them on alone." I tried to protest. "Now that we know they're working together, we need a plan to stop them." He grinned. "You know they're going to strike again, and next time, we'll finish off all of that cat's nine lives."

LOCATION: A top secret location in Miami Beach, Florida

Knock, knock, knock!

"Password?" I asked gruffly. I was trying to sound tough. After we arrived in Miami today, Kyle and I called a secret meeting with Jilly and Mikey G. to share what we found out about Bad Kitty (and to find out what Jilly was working on). Privacy was key.

"Password?" I heard Mikey G. grumble. "Why would *I* need a password? I'm the band's body-guard. My job is to be on the same side of the door as you guys, and you asked me to meet you here!"

He had a point.

Kyle opened the door for him, but Mikey G.

wasn't alone. Zander and Heath were with him, which was strictly against the rules of this meeting.

Mikey G. was calmly eating a WHEY OUT! bar. "Can we come in?"

I glared at Heath and Zander. "*You* can," I said to Mikey G. "Alone."

Heath dropped to his knees and proceeded to beg. "We're sorry we wigged out on you. We know we were wrong." He touched his head. "Look, I even dyed my hair turquoise because it's your favorite color."

"Kyle texted us about what happened," Zander said, and I looked at Kyle, who smiled weakly. Zander held out a bouquet of gorgeous orange, yellow, and red wildflowers I recognized from a display in the lobby. "We should have known you would never betray us." He batted his eyelashes at me. "I mean, you once told me you were Perfect Storm's biggest fan and knew everything there was to know about me, so I'm hoping that's still true."

Grrr...I hated how often Zander liked to bring that up. "And yet somehow you forgot that last night," I reminded him.

"Well, you're not completely innocent," Zander pointed out. "You did lose your journal long enough for Thunder and Lightning to steal Kyle's song."

"Allegedly," Kyle pointed out.

"Probably," Zander countered, "and that blows because, dude, your song was amazing and the perfect first single for our new album. That's probably why I've been so stressed about Thunder and Lightning. I hate them getting anything that awesome."

Kyle's grin exploded like fireworks. "Thanks, mate. That's decent of you to say."

"We're a team; we've got to have each other's backs," Heath agreed. "But we wouldn't be where we are without our friends, and Mac is one of the most loyal ones we've got." He was still on his knees. "We know you would never do anything

257

to hurt us on purpose. That would be like Iron Man being against Captain America."

"Um, isn't that the whole premise of the Civil War comic series?" I asked.

Heath's hands dropped to his sides. "I forgot about those. Bad example."

"The point is, we were wrong and you were right," Zander said. "Now we just want to help you take down Bad Kitty and save our reputation." He ran his hand through his hair. "If only we knew who she was."

"Has anyone seen Jilly?" I asked, and sent another WHERE ARE U???? text. The guys shrugged. Where could she be?

"So do you forgive us, O Comic Book Goddess, best friend and tour mate ever?" Heath clung to the bottom of my tank top. Zander dropped to his knees and started begging, too, which is something I never thought I'd see.

"Please, Mac? PLEEEEASE?" Zander sang. Heath joined in harmony.

"I forgive you!" I said with a laugh. Heath and Zander practically tackled me. Kyle dived over, too, and they made what they called a Mac sandwich.

"Now that you're mates again, let's get everyone up-to-date on what we do know," Kyle suggested, closing the door to the room to give us all some privacy.

We were meeting in the rooftop lounge of Blue, our hotel in Miami. Kyle got permission to take it over by telling the hotel manager he needed to practice singing a top secret song in private. (Kyle also gave the manager tickets to tomorrow night's show for his kids.) With floor-to-ceiling glass windows that overlooked Biscayne Bay and comfy leather furniture, the lounge was a relaxing oasis. But today it was our command bunker. With Jilly still MIA and not answering texts, Kyle and I filled everyone in. We taped up a timeline from the night at the recording studio when my journal first went missing to last night, when we spied Jeremy and Bad Kitty taking my journal off our tour bus. Scarlet and Iris joined us on speak-erphone to weigh in after e-mailing us all of Bad Kitty's vlogs on Perfect Storm.

"Hi!" Iris said nervously. "I just wanted to say it feels nice to be included, and I feel like we can really contribute to the conversation because I read everything there is to read about Zander—I mean, Welling. I mean, the band!"

Zander was too focused on Bad Kitty to real-ize what Iris had said. "Okay, people. Let's stop Bad Kitty. What do we know?"

Mikey G. tossed the WHEY OUT! bar he was eating into the nearest trash. "I know I'll never eat another one of these babies again. I can't believe they were sending me my favorite pro-tein bars as a trap! How did they know the WHEY OUT! bars case was so heavy I had to leave the bus unlocked to carry them in? I was only gone a few minutes!"

"And that's when they'd strike," Heath admitted. "It's pretty clever of them to send the big guy snacks and then use the delivery time to sneak on the bus." He scratched his turquoise head. "I'll have to remember that one."

"I've failed Bodyguarding 101," Mikey G. moaned. "Mac, you trusted me with your journal, and I failed you."

"You didn't know what they were up to." I hugged him so tight I didn't hear the door to the lounge open. "They tricked you. Now we can't put my journal back or they'll read this and know I'm on to them." I paused. "But if we don't put the

journal back, they'll know we know and we can't catch them." This was getting complicated.

"I just don't get how they knew I had your journal and that it was in the DVD case in the first place," Mikey G. complained.

"They knew because someone overheard you say it that night at the Beacon." Jilly rushed into the room with a stack of papers in her hands. "And I know who."

"Who?" we all cried.

"Lola!" Jilly said gleefully. "Remember when Mikey G. had thrown her out of that first concert for not having a confidentiality agreement signed?" I nodded. "We went out the same door to talk about Mac's journal. I'm pretty positive Lola overheard us."

"Impossible. Why didn't we spot her?" Mikey G. asked.

"We didn't spot her because she was wearing this!" Jilly slapped a photo of a girl in a black hoodie down on the table.

"Bad Kitty!" I exclaimed. "Wait, are you saying…?"

"YEP!" Jilly bounced up and down excitedly. "Lola Cummings is Bad Kitty!"

Everyone started talking at once while Scarlet and Iris were yelling into the speakerphone ("What's happening?"). Jilly whistled to get our attention.

"This is how I know," she said, and produced another piece of paper. "Lola is the one who e-mailed *Popstar!* magazine." We stared at the offensive e-mail that claimed I was the one leaking all the band's secrets. "That editor was lying when she said she didn't know who sent the e-mails." She threw up her hands and grinned. "When Jeremy got thrown from the bull at the photo shoot, I looked at the message she'd printed and memorized the e-mail address. Then I had a tech guy at Rock Starz find out where the e-mail came from, and, voilà, Bad Kitty is Lola Cummings."

"You traced the e-mail?" Heath asked. "Impressive. You're like a real spy."

"I just don't get why Lola would turn on us," Zander said. "She loves me—I mean us—I mean me. She follows the band to every city. She's a huge fan."

"Yeah, but you haven't been treating her like your biggest fan lately," Scarlet weighed in. "And knowing Lola, that was probably the problem."

"We did tell her that job was already taken—by Mac," Iris added.

We were all silent for a moment. "So do you think Lola did this because she was jealous of me?" I wondered aloud. I was completely shocked.

"It kind of makes sense," Jilly

said. "We always teased Lola that you were PS's biggest fan; and the last few times we saw her, the guys didn't give her the time of day. She must have been steamed."

"But she was so nice to me that day at Hurricane Harbor," Zander pointed out.

"She was probably trying to dig up more dirt," Jilly guessed.

"What's that jerk Jeremy got to do with any of this, though?" Heath asked. "Why would he team up with Lola?"

"I know the answer to that question, too. Cody!" Jilly yelled. "You can come in now."

Cody Callum walked into the lounge!

"No way! I don't trust this guy," Heath said. "I don't care what he told you."

"Just hear him out," Jilly said. "I already interrogated him, and I believe him."

Wow, Jilly really was a secret agent. Amazing.

"Jeremy was really mad you ignored us that night at SoundEscape," Cody said. "We were really nervous about our demo, and you guys just blew us off when we asked for your advice."

"Dude, we'd been recording for over ten hours," Heath said. "We were toast."

"We still could have talked to them," Kyle realized. "Remember when we got our big break? The least we could have done was give them a few minutes." He looked at Cody. "I'm sorry, mate. But that still doesn't give Jeremy the right to tear us down."

"I knew he and Lola were talking trash about you guys, but I had no idea they had taken things this far," Cody said. "I feel so stupid. One time I even saw him coming off your bus, but when I asked what he was doing, he said he was returning something he borrowed. I guess it became easier for me to just let Jeremy do his thing." Cody stared at the floor. "I hate when he gets mad at me."

"Why didn't you tell us he was sneaking around our bus?" Heath demanded.

"Jeremy's my brother," Cody said. "Things

had gotten so bad. I had to take a side, and I chose his." He looked miserable. "But I always felt bad about Kyle's song. I swear I didn't know the song was stolen! I thought it was weird how we got it right before we had to record the demo, but Jeremy wouldn't tell me who gave it to him." He looked up. "WAIT. I just remembered something." Cody locked eyes with Kyle. "Jeremy was talking to a girl outside our recording studio the night we met you guys. She gave him a piece of paper, and I thought it was her phone number!" He hung his head sadly. "It must have been Kyle's lyrics. I'm such an idiot."

Heath leaned against the window. "Wow. And I was starting to think The Raven gave him Kyle's song. He never liked it—no offense—and he kept pushing for a different single. But it was Lola!"

"We can't trust anyone anymore," Zander said mournfully.

"I should have told you sooner," Cody said.

The Story of
a Girl

See her standing there
in her messed-up kicks,
Looking like she's got
the whole world to fix,
With a smile that feels
like a million watts
And a laugh that makes
me wanna rock.
(chorus)
Oh! She's a hero in
I'll be forever wait
Continued →

Thought this would be perfect for you 😊

"I never wanted any of this—touring, record deals, my name all over blogs and Twitter. I just wanted to write music, but Ronald said a duo was stronger than a solo artist, so Jeremy begged me to do this with him."

"You want to write songs?" Kyle asked quietly.

Cody nodded. "I like arranging music more than writing words. What you wrote is gold, and I'm sorry we took it from you. I've been trying to come up with something better ever since, but songwriting is much harder than I thought it would be. You can't come up with a new song every day, can you?"

"No, you can't," Kyle said, but he didn't sound angry. He sort of sounded like he understood what Cody meant. "I've been struggling to come up with a single as good as the one I already wrote for over a month now, but blimey, it's tough."

"Maybe we could try doing something together," Cody suggested.

"That's so nice," Jilly said, and I noticed her staring at Cody in that same way she had when we first met him. "But that doesn't change the fact that we can't get Kyle's song back—the label would never let them record it now. The only thing we can do is try to stop Lola from ever vlogging about Perfect Storm again."

"Whatever we do, we have to be careful," Iris said. "We have no idea how many other things Mac's written about that Lola's holding to use. I'm sure Jeremy is just egging Lola on more."

"Let's face it." I sank into the nearest armchair and covered my face with one of the decorative pillows. "The only choice I have is to stop writing in my journal for good. As it is, I'm writing in a replacement journal so they don't read these posts."

"Mac, no!" Jilly cried. "You love your journal."

"You said it inspires your *Mac Attack* comics!" Scarlet added. "You can't stop writing."

"If you do that, then you're letting Big Bird Cummings win," Jilly said angrily.

"You can write about me all you want," Kyle said. "I don't care what that cat says about us. Our loyal fans will know the truth."

"Yeah, but do they have to know *everything* about us?" Heath asked nervously. "Those stuff-a-bear places have been calling all week, asking me to be their new spokesperson." The rest of us started to laugh as his cheeks continued to redden. "It's embarrassing."

"What if I write some lies about Perfect Storm

in my original journal?" I suggested. "Bad Kitty would look like a fool if we could prove they were false."

"Too risky. We don't need any more bad publicity," Heath said.

Gotcha. This morning Iris forwarded a gossip column that said Heath had brushed his teeth with a toothbrush that fell in the toilet. It's true. I saw it happen. But maybe I shouldn't have, um, written about it.

POPST☆R.com

HEATH USES TOILET TOOTHBRUSH TO BRUSH TEETH

Think twice before kissing him!

"What if you wrote about a mean prank we were going to play on Thunder and Lightning?" Kyle said, thinking aloud. "And said exactly when and where it was going to happen. Then they'd probably show up to record the whole thing, and we could catch Lola in the act."

"Now we're talking," Heath said eagerly. "But what about Jeremy?"

"You could stake out your tour bus to get pictures of them stealing your journal," Cody suggested.

"You want to help us take down Jeremy?" Jilly asked. "Won't your brother be mad?"

"It's the least I can do after we took your song," Cody said. "I owe you guys. I can help. Lola's dad is coming to town tomorrow to see our set at the show. If you set the prank to happen before the concert, her dad would be backstage and see for himself how his daughter is trying to ruin the reputation of a band he sponsors."

"This is brill," said Heath, stealing Kyle's favorite word.

"Do you really think we can pull this off?" Jilly asked.

I scratched my chin. Mac Attack could do it, which meant so could we. "I think we can. Everyone in favor of Operation Take Down Bad Kitty?" I put my hand in, and everyone piled their hands on top while Iris and Scarlet yelled their support from the phone. "That cat goes down tomorrow!"

Ring, ring, ring.

"Madam Celeste, your eyes on the future, speaking!"

"Is this THE Madam Celeste of Stone Harbor, New Jersey, next to the frozen-custard stand in the tiny alleyway?" I asked hopefully.

"Yes, this is she," Madam Celeste said in the smoky voice I wouldn't soon forget. It haunted my dreams even more than *The Sharkinator Returns*. "Are you looking to make an appointment, dearie? I have three, three forty-five, four, four thirty—"

"I found you!" I cheered, cutting Madam Celeste off. "You have no idea how many Madam Celeste psychics there are in the New Jersey beach towns. I called six before I remembered you were in Stone Harbor. Listen, about the psychic reading you did for me..."

Madam Celeste exhaled. "No refunds on readings, dearie. It's on my sign. Now, if you'll excuse me, I should go meditate."

"No, wait!" I begged. "I don't want a refund. I just had a question."

"Oh, okay," Madam Celeste said. "That will be fourteen dollars and ninety-five cents for a phone session, plus your regular calling fees."

"I..." I searched my pockets for cash. "Do I mail you the money? I'm too young for a credit card, and I'm not sure how my mom will feel about my borrowing hers for a phone psychic reading." I could see Mom from where I sat on a crate of new Sizzling Summer Boys Tour merchandise, backstage at Blue's concert venue.

I'd never met a Perfect Storm tee I hadn't liked before, but this one had both Perfect Storm and Thunder and Lightning on it. There was no way I was wearing that.

Madam Celeste exhaled deeply again. "Fine. One question on the house."

My heart sped up. "You said during my reading that you could see a perfect storm coming for me, but you didn't say how to, um, end the storm or…" Gee, I had no clue what I actually wanted to know. "Whether I could, um, survive the storm? Maybe all I need is an umbrella? Or rain boots? I always wanted purple ones with little pink hearts on them."

Madam Celeste started to laugh. "Dearie, my saying a storm is coming, if that's what I said, just means a heap of trouble is headed your way. You don't need an actual umbrella."

"No, I know that, but all you said was 'A storm is coming,'" I repeated. I saw Mikey G. walk by and give me a thumbs-up. Zander and Heath hurried behind him with a box of glue and feathers. This was going to be good. "You didn't say how I could stop the storm."

Madam Celeste huffed. "This is what Madam Eugenie meant by my predictions being negative. Look at how you've clung to this reading I don't even remember! If you were here today—or paying for this phone session—I could dive deeper into what was going on in your life, but since you can't, I'll just say this: Storms pass. The key is weathering the storm with friends. It's always better than doing it alone. You get what I'm saying, dearie?"

Kyle and Jilly were lugging a huge fan. They saw me and stopped. "I think so." Madam Celeste was telling me what I knew all along. "Thanks, Madam Celeste! See you next time I'm in Stone Harbor." I hung up while she was in the middle of explaining her weekly telephone reading options. Mom would kill me. "Nice fan," I said to Kyle.

"Cowards should be tarred and feathered," Kyle said with a wink. "I'm so glad we went with the prank my mates always pulled at boarding school."

It was pretty perfect. Kyle dictated it to me so I had it right in my journal. Jeremy and Cody will walk through a door pulled so tight with plastic wrap covered in glue that they won't even see it there. Then we'll turn on the fan. They'll be covered with feathers when they take the stage and look like giant chickens, which is what Jeremy is for not coming clean about stealing PS's song!

Jilly checked her watch. "We better go set up. We have less than an hour till showtime. If all goes as planned, Daddy will be here with Lola's dad in time to see this all go down."

The walkie-talkie in Jilly's hand crackled to life.

"This is Curly, Turquoise, and WHEY OUT! checking in with the Lovebirds and the Bean."

The voice sounded like Heath, who I was sure was Turquoise. Curly had to be Zander, Jilly had to be the Bean (for Jilly Bean), and Mikey G. was WHEY OUT!, which meant Kyle and I were the Lovebirds. Well, that was awkward.

"You coming or what?" Heath asked. "It's go time!"

Jilly grabbed the walkie-talkie. "Ready! Bring-ing the fan over now."

The three of us dragged the fan through the backstage area. After all the pranks that had gone down on the road, the roadies were on to us, but I doubted they would try to stop us. While we were walking around, we passed Cody on the phone and paused to listen to his conversation.

"You read what?" I heard Cody say. "Tonight? There's no way— Wait. I see Kyle backstage, and he's carrying a huge fan. And Mac and Jilly have feathers! Maybe you're right. I think that prank is going down tonight." Cody paused to listen. "Why didn't I think of that, Jer? If Bad Kitty catches them in the act, they're toast. Yes! She should definitely record the prank. Even better, what if she reported live from the prank?"

"Jeremy and Lola bought it!" Jilly said excitedly.

"Exactly," Cody said into the phone. "Bad Kitty will record the whole thing, and the whole world will feel bad for us." Cody waved us away, and we ran past him. There was no time to lose. We had to get in position. The guys were set to go on in ten.

"Any sign of our cat?" Zander asked when we made our way to the others. He was hanging another box of feathers above the doorway on a ladder ready to trip when the plastic wrap was pulled down. "I haven't seen Lola yet, but that doesn't mean she's not already here." I could picture Lola in her Bad Kitty getup hiding behind some sound equipment recording us already.

All the guys looked anxious. If this prank

worked, we'd expose Lola as Bad Kitty. If it went wrong, then it would make Perfect Storm look bad. Already I'd heard some of the crew complaining about the pranks. I even heard one guy say he wished the tour was over. We had three more stops, but I had a feeling that if tonight went as planned, Thunder and Lightning wouldn't be on them.

"Thunder and Lightning is on in ten!" the backstage manager announced. He stopped short when he saw Heath standing on a ladder with feathers. He shook his head and walked away.

"Places, everyone," Heath said, and we got into position. Heath on the ladder with the feathers, Zander ready to pull the fan, and Kyle holding a bottle of glue. Jilly and I were on the phone with Iris and Scarlet (who were on the phone with us so they could hear what was happening. Iris even had Bad Kitty's vlog up to see if she would post anything). Then we heard Jeremy holler a greeting to everyone backstage.

"Hello, Miami Beach! Thunder and Lightning is here!" Jeremy said. I wondered why he was being so loud in announcing himself. Then I realized: Lola was definitely hiding backstage somewhere. I could only hope her hiding spot was exactly where we thought it would be.

"Her vlog is live-streaming!" Iris whispered, as if someone at the concert could hear her through the phone. "Bad Kitty is reporting live from backstage at the concert and— OH MY GOD, MAC, I can totally see you. She's standing just feet away from you!"

Bingo! This was going to work. It had to.

I glanced out of the corner of my eye. There was Lola behind the giant Perfect Storm sign that would be wheeled out onstage before the guys' act.

"So do we head onstage this way?" Jeremy asked loudly, walking on purpose toward the doorway with the plastic wrap. "Gee, what's this here?"

"NOW!" Heath shouted, and pulled a cord above Jeremy and Cody. Nothing happened.

"What's going on?" Jeremy asked, wiping glue from his face and pulling the plastic wrap away. He kept looking up for the feathers that didn't fall. "I thought you guys were—"

Then we heard a high-pitched scream. Glue and feathers were raining down, but not on Jeremy and Cody. They were falling on Lola! Gotcha! My journal hadn't mentioned that we had set up the prank in an alternate spot to catch Lola.

"My clothes!" I heard her shout. "Someone help me! I've been feathered!"

Jilly and I ran over, and Jilly pulled back Lola's hood while I grabbed her phone, which was still recording. I turned the video on her so her viewers could see what was going on.

"Hi, Bad Kitty!" Jilly said, holding on to Lola's hoodie so she couldn't get away. "Or should we call you Lola Cummings?"

Lola squirmed. "I don't know what you're talking about!"

"Sure, you do," I said as Heath dragged a sticky Jeremy and Cody over to the camera.

"You've been vlogging as Bad Kitty for the last few weeks!" Jilly said. "You've been saying horrible things about Perfect Storm because you were jealous that they didn't think you were their number one fan."

Ronald raced around the corner, saw the scene, and stopped short. "What's happening?"

Lola spit out a feather. "I...we...they...Zander...Jeremy...," she stuttered. Her eyes narrowed at me. "I *am* their number one fan! At least I was until you came along and ruined everything!" she screamed. "Because of you, the guys ignore me!"

"So you turned on us?" Zander asked. "We love all our fans the same," he said to the camera. "We're sorry if we can't give all of you the attention you deserve. There are not enough hours in the day to tell you how much we love you guys, but we do."

I heard Scarlet and Iris say "Aww."

"We adore our fans, and the best way to show that is by touring and recording songs you'll love," Zander said. "Anyone who tells you otherwise is a liar."

"Bad Kitty/Lola, your gig is up," Heath said. "We were never planning to prank Thunder and Lightning." He looked at the brothers.

"Jeremy, you've been a pain this whole tour, and your punishment is admitting to the label that you've been feeding secrets about us to Bad Kitty."

"You can't prove that!" Jeremy sputtered as one of Lola's feathers flew into his mouth. Outside, I could hear the concert venue filling up with fans. The show would be starting late, if it started at all.

"Yes, they can," Cody said quietly. "We took photos of you and Lola on the tour bus stealing Mac's journal again this afternoon. We also have proof that Lola is Bad Kitty and has been using what's in Mac's journal on her vlog. And you helped her the whole time."

"Jeremy, you didn't!" Ronald held his head in his hands. "You guys are on the same label. How could you?"

"I wonder what your dad would say, Lola, about what you've been up to," Jilly said smugly. "Oh, look! He's here! Hi, Mr. Cummings!"

Briggs, Mom, and Lola's dad stopped short

when they saw the glue and feathers all over the floor.

"What the— Lola?" Lola's dad asked when he saw her. He looked nothing like his daughter. He was much shorter, and he had on a Wave One tee and jeans.

"Do you want to tell him what's going on or should we?" Jilly crossed her arms.

Lola just scowled silently.

"Fine, I'll do it," Jilly said. "Lola's been vlogging as Bad Kitty to destroy Perfect Storm's reputation. If their reputation is ruined, then so is your investment in their tour."

"You're Bad Kitty?" Her dad's mouth widened into a large O. "Wave One has been freaking out over the potential loss of ticket sales and media issues and...and..." He was getting madder and madder. "LOLA PINKIE CUMMINGS! You're being sent to Grandma's farm in Nebraska to work all summer as punishment!"

"No!" Lola sobbed. "Not the farm! Anything but feeding pigs."

"Pinkie?" Jilly and I repeated as Scarlet and Iris did the same through the phone. Mom took Lola's phone from my hands and stopped recording.

"What do you say we keep this matter between us," Briggs offered to Mr. Cummings soothingly. "Well, between us and the viewers of your daughter's live vlog. We won't press charges," he told Ronald. "Your boys already recorded Kyle's song, and Kyle is receiving royalties, but I think it's for the best if you leave the tour tonight."

"Wait, we don't even get to go on?" Jeremy cried. "This is ridiculous! Perfect Storm takes everything!"

"No, we work for what we've got," Heath said, throwing an arm around Kyle and Zander, "and no vlogger or rip-off band is going to change what we have together."

"Lola, you're coming with me." Mr. Cummings pulled Lola away from Jilly's grasp. "I'll take you to Nebraska personally tonight."

Lola whimpered. "I hate pigs."

"Bye, Pinkie!" I sang. "We'll miss you!"

"No, we won't," Heath told her as we waved. Ronald grabbed Jeremy and pulled him away to presumably yell at him, too.

And that is how you put a bad kitty in her place!

"So Thunder and Lightning are not going on?" a bewildered roadie asked.

"Perfect Storm will do a longer set," Mom suggested. "Just reset. It may take a half hour." She glanced at her phone for the time.

"Can I run out onstage and explain to the fans what's happening?" Zander asked. Mom nodded. "I'll tell them we'll be out in a bit to give them a concert they won't soon forget."

Kyle put out his hand to shake Cody's. "Thanks for your help, mate. It couldn't have been easy to rat out your brother like that."

Cody shrugged. "It felt pretty good, actually."

He laughed. "Jeremy has been bossing me around for years. I'm sorry about your song, though."

"I'll write a better one," Kyle said, and looked at me. "I actually have some ideas right now, in fact. Anyone got a pen?" he asked.

"Want some help?" Cody asked. "Least I could do."

"Why not?" Kyle said with a smile. "Meet you in the greenroom in five."

"Awesome," Cody said, and then turned to Jilly. "I'm sorry we started out on the wrong foot."

"Then let's start over." Jilly extended her hand. "Hi. I'm Jillian Pepper, daughter of Briggs Pepper, Perfect Storm's manager."

Cody smiled. "Cody Callum, future song-writer and brother of Jeremy Callum, who may or may not still have a career in music."

I smiled. The storm had passed, for now at least, and it would be smooth sailing for the rest of the tour.

293

Monday, July 11 (It's one AM!!!)

LOCATION: On the tour bus outside El Tortilla Factory Restaurant in Miami Beach, Florida—POST-VICTORY PARTY!

Operation Take Down Bad Kitty was a total success!

We were so excited, we had to celebrate, which is why, after Perfect Storm played a SOLO concert, we headed to El Tortilla Factory. The restaurant was near closing, but Briggs persuaded them to stay open. He even got the mariachi band to keep playing, and Perfect Storm jammed with them. None of us wanted to go back to the hotel yet. Mom, Briggs, Mikey G., PS, Jilly, me, some of the roadies, and even Cody were still ordering guacamole and eating tortilla chips and fried ice cream. Briggs was finally taking Iris's advice and having PS go on The Morning Mash Up in the AM to talk to Nicole, Ryan, and Stanley T. so they could give them the full scoop on what happened with Thunder and Lightning. We were all in a celebratory mood because WE WON!

Heath, in an oversize straw hat, was leading a conga line with a pair of mariachis, when Kyle pulled me out of the line to talk to me.

"I have a present for you," he yelled over the singing and rattling from the mariachis.

"WHAT?" I shouted back because I couldn't hear him well at first.

Kyle took me to a corner of the outdoor seating area where there was a fountain and hanging twinkling lights. It was really pretty.

"I said, I have a present for you," Kyle repeated, and then he offered me a box wrapped with polka-dot paper.

Kyle had bought me a present? My knees felt like they might give out and not because the small rectangular box was heavy. What could it be?

"Thank you!" I quickly unwrapped the box and gasped. It was a silver case with an electronic keypad on it. "You got me a lockbox for my journal?"

"Actually, it's a lockbox that is a journal," Kyle said. "It has a safelike coating that keeps anyone from cracking it open, and you seal it with a combination that you change every month. I know you love the journal you had, but I thought you might feel safer with this one."

I stared at my new journal (which is what I'm writing in now!) and was in total awe. "This is the nicest thing anybody has ever given me. Thank you."

"I'm sorry we were so hard on you about Thunder and Lightning," Kyle said. "I know you would never do anything to hurt our band, Mac."

Now I was feeling misty. I would not cry in front of Kyle. I would NOT cry in front of Kyle! "You guys are the most amazing band in the world," I said, and he blushed. "I would never EVER do anything to hurt you guys. I want to see you take over the world."

"Well, maybe with this new song, we can," Kyle said, and he whistled to someone. I watched Cody walk toward us with the mariachi band in tow. "Now, it's pretty rough, since Cody and I just wrote this a few hours ago, but I still think it's brill. I'm calling it 'Unstoppable,' because that's

302

what you are." Kyle took a guitar from one of the mariachi guys while Cody took a pair of maracas. Then the two sang the most beautiful ballad I've ever heard. Briggs, Mom, Zander, Heath, and Jilly walked over, too.

"Looked across the room that night
I saw you standing there beneath the light,
A shadow cast across your smile.
Took a chance, walked up to you,
Looked in your eyes, and it was then that I knew
We'd be standing here together.
Together we'll be unstoppable
Anything we wanna be
Together you'll see we'll be unstoppable
You and me."

They sang one more verse, but I was in such shock that I don't think I heard it. All I heard were the words "together" and "unstoppable." Together. Did that mean Kyle could see a future in Paris with me, too? I glanced at Mom, who was smiling. There was no way this dream would happen tonight, or tomorrow, or a hundred tomorrows from now, but it could happen someday.

"So? What do you think?" Kyle looked nervous.

"I think it's aces and brill all wrapped into one," I said breathlessly.

"Me too, man!" Heath clapped. "That's the song we've been looking for."

"Me too, but, um, Cody's not actually going to

sing on it, is he?" Zander asked, trying to sound nonchalant.

We all laughed.

"No, man," Cody said. "We're waiting to hear back from the label on what's next, but I know for me, I want to be a songwriter, and writing for you guys is the best gig I could ever get."

"This calls for a toast!" Mom announced.

"To Perfect Storm!" Jilly held up a glass. "Their new single is going to be the hottest thing on the charts!"

"Here, here!" Briggs seconded.

"And to friends like Mac and Jilly, who always have Perfect Storm's back!" Zander added.

"Don't forget Scarlet and Iris," Heath added. I knew they'd love hearing that.

"And Cody," Kyle added. "You're a good writing partner." The two clinked glasses.

"Let's conga!" Heath declared, and the mariachi band encouraged everyone to join in. The others jumped in line, but I was lost in my own thoughts. Ones where Perfect Storm was the hugest boy band in the world and I spent the next few years touring with them, just like I was right now. Together we would be unstoppable, just like Kyle's song said. Maybe Paris wasn't so far off in the future...

"Mac?" I looked up and saw Kyle reaching out for my hand. The conga line was heading our way. "Want to dance?"

"I'd love to!" I grabbed Kyle's hand and let him lead me to the back of the conga line.

When it came to Perfect Storm, I knew we could weather anything that came our way.

ACKNOWLEDGMENTS

Whether it's a music tour like Perfect Storm's or a book like VIP: *Battle of the Bands*, it takes a LOT of people behind the scenes to make it happen! Thank you to VIP's road manager (sorry, Mac's mom!), Pam Gruber, my awesome editor; and Kristina Aven, VIP's publicist, for keeping the series' name in lights. Shout-outs to the rest of the LBYR crew—Andrew Smith, Melanie Chang, Leslie Shumate, Maggie Edkins, Wendy Dopkin, and Tracy Koontz—for all they do.

To illustrator Kristen Gudsnuk: I suspect we would have gone to many *NSYNC concerts together if we had known each other as teens! Thank you for having Mac's back and for bringing her and the Perfect Storm gang to life in such an incredible way.

Dan Mandel, you are a true headliner. Thanks for helping Mac and me have the best time on this road trip.

No tour would be complete without backstage passes, and I have to give them out to boy-band guru Elizabeth Eulberg as well as Kieran Scott, Jennifer E. Smith, Katie Sise, Tiffany Schmidt, and Courtney Sheinmel for all their writerly advice.

Special thanks to my friend Rick Delucia for lending me his song "Unstoppable" for *VIP: Battle of the Bands*. It's the perfect song for Kyle, and I'm so fortunate to have a talented friend who can write lyrics!

And to my tour-bus mates—Mike, Tyler, Dylan (and, of course, Jack): Thanks for going on this crazy ride with me. It's because of you guys—the fab four—that I can do what I do, and I love you all for it.